He heard it in the disdain in her voice, saw it in the fiery darts shooting from her eyes. The word "savage" was so clearly embedded in her mind, it could have been engraved on her forehead. A searing arrow of rage shot through him. He released her so abruptly, she stumbled backward. When she fell, landing on her backside, he fought the instinctive urge to reach for her.

She braced herself with her palms on the ground, a few inches behind her hips, and glowered up at him. "You despicable man."

Her blatant description of him almost took him aback. "Savage" he knew how to deal with, from experience. But he'd never been called despicable before. He felt she thought him vile instead of barbaric.

He preferred barbaric.

Swiftly, he changed the direction of his thoughts. What did he care what she thought of him? She wasn't a person of consequence to his life. Never would be.

Deciding his next practical move was to get her home, he reached down his hand to her. She ignored his gesture, scrambling up on her own, which didn't surprise him. He dropped his hand back to his side.

Looking down, she adjusted her cloak. The visible trembling in her hands betrayed how shaken she still was.

Ethan's emotions weighed equally between irritation and regret. Didn't she realize if he meant her any harm, the deed would be done by now? "What do you think I'm going to do, Miss Gunter? Scalp you? Hang my bounty out in the sun to dry?"

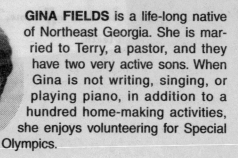

GINA FIELDS is a life-long native of Northeast Georgia. She is married to Terry, a pastor, and they have two very active sons. When Gina is not writing, singing, or playing piano, in addition to a hundred home-making activities, she enjoys volunteering for Special Olympics.

Books by Gina Fields

HEARTSONG PRESENTS
HP262—Heaven's Child
HP289—The Perfect Wife
HP365—Still Waters
HP389—Familiar Strangers

Spirit
of the Eagle

Gina Fields

Heartsong Presents

Dedicated to Blake,
I'm proud of you, my son.
Love, Mom

Special thanks to:
Johnny Chattin, for sharing your heritage with me;
and to Bill Kinsland of the Hometown Bookstore,
for answering my many research questions.

A note from the author:
*I love to hear from my readers! You may correspond with me
by writing:*
                          Gina Fields
                          Author Relations
                          PO Box 719
                          Uhrichsville, OH 44683

ISBN 1-58660-150-4

SPIRIT OF THE EAGLE

All Scripture quotations are taken from the King James Version of
the Bible.

Cover illustration by Lauraine Bush.

PRINTED IN THE U.S.A.

one

Ethan Walker glanced out the open double doors of his grist-mill and saw from the absence of shadows the sun set high in the sky. He dropped his scoop into the half-full barrel of corn-meal and slid the heavy lid over the mouth of the wooden drum. He then tied a rope around the open end of the cloth sack leaning heavily against his leg, hoisted the one-hundred-pound bag of meal to his shoulder, and carried the sack to the back storeroom, where he laid it on top of several other bags.

Grain supplies were getting low. It would soon be time for planting to replenish the storehouse. And they *would* plant; the ground was already being prepared. But this year, he knew, his people would not be here to see the crops through to harvest.

Still, he would encourage his family and neighbors to plant. They needed something to hold on to until the day appointed for enforcement of the unsanctioned Treaty of New Echota which would force all Cherokees to move west beyond the Mississippi.

As he sauntered back through the packing room, he retrieved his homespun shirt from atop another barrel. Slipping one arm and then the other into the full sleeves, he stepped out into the crisp March air. The spirited breeze fingered his sweat-dampened face and meal-dusty chest, offering a welcome reprieve from the stagnant air trapped within the mill's walls.

He paused, fastening the cuff buttons on his sleeves, and looked around him. To his right, a small waterfall in the Chestatee River, the power source for his mill, rumbled like distant thunder over the riverbed rocks. The budding oak, maple, and laurel branches that hovered above the rushing water were alive with birdsong, squirrel dances, and the breath of the wind. To his far left lay the newly-turned red earth of the planting fields. Beyond those fields, the three homes of his neighbors dotted the landscape.

Looking straight ahead, where the river took a southward bend, his gaze fell upon two log houses. One was the home of his mother's cousin, Jim Walker, and his family. The other, the larger of the two, Ethan's grandfather had built. It was the house where his mother had lived—the house where he and his siblings had been born, as were his sister's children—the house that he, for twenty-six years, had called home.

He swallowed past the tightness growing in his throat. Everything within Ethan's sight was all that was left of his once prosperous village.

There were other houses in the Cherokee nation that were still occupied by his people: humble shacks tucked in out-of-the-way mountain coves that were of little interest to the gold miners who had flooded North Georgia over the past ten years. Then, there were those Cherokee who had been allowed to remain in their homes because they had betrayed their own by pledging loyalty to the treaty.

But the majority of the Cherokee homes either now stood vacant, were occupied by whites, or burned to rubble, the owners having been illegally driven out by "fortunate drawers" of a land lottery—or so the government had called it. The Cherokee called it robbery.

Ethan's own family and few neighbors would be gone, too, if not for the kindness and generosity of one white man.

As Ethan lifted his eyes to the blue-hued mountains along the horizon, a great, desolate heaviness bore down on his chest. His people had hunted those hills long before his grandfather's time. They had planted in the fertile valleys, fished in the bountiful streams. They had been a free people in a free land.

Then the intruders had come with their modern ways and

misguided idealism. "Learn our ways," they had said. "Make a better life for yourself."

The simmering anger that had been Ethan's constant companion for months now broke free and lashed across his chest. He curled his hands into tight fists at his side. His people had learned the white man's ways, welcomed him into their homes, even into their families. And what had it gotten them? A divided nation, wounded spirits, the loss of their freedom. . .

Betrayed trust.

Ethan closed his eyes against the grief that threatened to choke him. For ten years, he'd witnessed the rapid decline of his nation. In two months, he'd see its complete demise. Where was the God his family believed in and so loyally prayed to each day? Even He, it seemed, had forsaken them.

"Uncle Ethan, do you want to play?"

His young nephew's voice penetrated Ethan's harrowing thoughts. Carefully masking his anger, he opened his eyes and shifted his gaze toward the side of Jim's smaller cabin, where four young children—three boys and one girl—had gathered for a lively game of stickball.

Ethan raised his hand in greeting. "Not now, Jedidiah. I have something I must do first."

They accepted his answer without argument and went on with their energetic game. Within seconds, dust from the barren playing field churned around their feet like angry red clouds as they passed a deerskin ball back and forth with sticks that had been fashioned with webs of beaver hide on one end.

Buttoning his shirt and tucking in his shirttail, Ethan lumbered along the riverbank. When he was three arm spans from the bridge that linked his homestead to the gold mining town of Adela, he turned, shuffled down the grassy slope, and crouched behind a laurel thicket. Here he could remain hidden from curious eyes across the river and still see all he needed to see.

Through the dense branches, he focused on the church that served as the white man's place of worship on Sunday and the white children's school during the week. Soon, the children would burst from the doors and run like wild boars through the red clay street to their various destinations.

Then, he need only wait a few more minutes before she would appear, the white woman with hair like moonbeams who had come from Virginia to teach the white children. When she walked home, she would, as always, take the path along the river. And, as always, she would stop at the bridge and look across to the field where his young kindred played.

Only today, stopping and watching would not be enough for her. Today, she would try to cross. Ethan knew because he had watched from this very spot for eight days now. Each day, he'd seen the desire in her eyes and the longing in her face grow. She wanted to teach the Cherokee children to read and write the English language. But the young Cherokee had no need of her instruction now, for they would soon be gone.

She knew it, too. For she now lived and worked among the very people who lay in wait like vultures to devour the remainder of his people's land—what meager portion there was left of it. But that wouldn't stop her. The desire in her eyes was too strong. It would not be easy to convince her that her efforts to help the Cherokee children would be in vain.

And dangerous.

Both for her and his family. The local vigilante pony clubs that roamed the backwoods seeking Cherokee to torture were not above terrorizing them in their own homes, along with anyone closely associated with them.

For that reason, he must stop her.

But the feeling in his gut told him it would not be easy.

❧

"Brian, I wouldn't do that, if I were you."

Immediately, the shuffling in the back of the classroom ceased.

"Remember," Lillian Gunter reminded the boy, "a written report is due on *The Spy* by the end of next week. It might be wise to keep reading."

She didn't bother lifting her eyes from the notebook in

which she was recording grades. During the three weeks she had been teaching in Adela, she had learned her eleven students well. She knew exactly what had just taken place. She could tell by the scuffing of feet and the muffled chuckles of her other male students in the back row. Thirteen-year-old Brian Hawkins had been in the process of reaching across the aisle to jerk one of Susie Preston's pigtails.

Would he never tire of teasing the young girl?

Mentally, Lillian shook her head. Probably not for several more years. If Lillian's instincts were not misleading her, Brian really was quite smitten with the pretty, little redhead, and he simply didn't know how else to gain her attention.

The corners of Lillian's mouth eased up as she entered an admirable grade next to Brian's name. She made a mental note to commend him later—confidentially, of course, so as not to embarrass the sensitive adolescent in front of his classmates. He was such a bright young man whenever he applied himself to his studies instead of the mischief he so often preferred.

"Hannah, do you have something you want to share with the rest of the class?"

The whispering that had commenced on the third row died away, and Lillian filtered a despondent sigh. Little Hannah Braden couldn't seem to keep her mind off talking and on her studies. The eight-year-old wasn't defiant or rebellious; she simply preferred idle conversation above instruction. Lillian hadn't yet figured out how to reroute the young girl's attention.

Lillian entered another grade in the notebook. Maybe she should write her former tutor in Virginia. The broad-minded instructor had been quite creative in finding ways to redirect Lillian's wandering young mind when she was a student, even if it meant taking the lessons outside to the green lawns of the plantation, which always appalled Lillian's mother. Pale skin was fashionable; golden skin was not.

Lillian felt the sharp sting of unbidden tears, and the numbers in the grade book blurred. Her mother had been gone eight months now, and still, Lillian sometimes found herself overcome with grief at the most inopportune times.

Not wanting the children to suspect her sudden attack of sorrow, she kept her fuzzy gaze fixed on the notebook. The last year had been a grievous one. Her mother's illness had been long and painful. And the entire time she was sitting at her sick mother's bedside, her fiancé was out having little romantic trysts with her best friend.

Lillian's cheeks burned with remembrance. She'd never forget the day she confronted James and he revealed her suspicions, nor the flippant way he'd told her he was in love with her most trusted childhood friend. A quick surge of anger shot through her. She'd never felt so betrayed—or humiliated—in her entire life. Everyone advised her to "get back out and socialize; get on with her life." But the last thing she'd wanted to do was step back out into the throes of society. She couldn't bear going to spring parties and social gatherings and seeing James walk in with Camille on his arm; nor could Lillian tolerate the whispers behind her back.

Her vision cleared enough for her to resume posting grades. When her Aunt Emma had written and asked Lillian if she'd consider the vacant teaching position in Adela, Lillian eagerly accepted. She saw her aunt's offer as an answered prayer that would meet two of her immediate needs: to get out of Wilmington for awhile, and to pursue her lifelong dream of teaching—a vocation her friends considered unsuitable for a lady of genteel upbringing.

Pursing her lips, she thought back to her father's reaction to her moving to North Georgia. Since tensions were running high over the upcoming deadline of the removal treaty, he had some misgivings. The Georgians were pushing for removal; the Cherokee were fighting it.

But as a missionary's son who'd lived among the Cherokee in his teens, her father knew they were a humble and peaceful people. If any trouble came, it would be from those of her own race who were campaigning for the removal. Since Lillian wasn't Cherokee, she would not be in the path of adversity. And Lillian would be staying with his sister,

Emma, and her husband, Reverend Frederick Price, had served as Adela's pastor for ten years now. Marcus knew his brother-in-law had compassion for the Cherokee and that Lillian would be safe in their home, sheltered from prejudice.

So, without much argument, he'd agreed to let her come. Not that she had needed his permission. But, if he'd asked her to stay and help the very capable housekeeper and foreman oversee the plantation's operations, she would have. Even at twenty, she respected her father's wishes.

She posted the last grade then lifted the timepiece dangling from an elegant gold chain she wore around her neck. Noon, dismissal time, was rapidly approaching. She started lessons promptly at eight each morning. Because parents insisted the children be home attending to chores after the midday meal, she released them promptly at noon, unless she was so engrossed in a lesson that had captured both her and the students' attention that she forgot the passing of time. That had happened twice since she had been here. Once, an alert student had reminded her of her oversight. The other time, a displeased farmer laboring to prepare his fields for planting had come to collect his son.

But today would not be one of those days. The children had worked diligently all morning, and she could tell from their growing restlessness they were ready for a break.

She laid aside her pencil, stood, and clasped her hands in front of her. "All right, class, I think that will be all for today. Since it's Friday, you need to leave your assignments, any extra paper you have, and your pencils in the crate on my desk as you leave."

Monday through Thursday, she allowed the children to keep materials at their desks. But on the weekends, the homemade desks were transferred to a makeshift storage room recently built near the church. Then the wooden benches, now stacked on the podium behind her teaching desk, were lined up in the sanctuary for Sunday meeting.

There was a clamor of desks, shoes, boots—and even a few

bare feet—scraping across the plank floor as the students hurried to deliver their assignments to the crate and rush out into the bright sunshine. To her good fortune, Brian fell in line last. Along with the papers he turned in, he included the James Fennimore Cooper novel Lillian had assigned him to read.

"Brian."

When he stopped in the open doorway and turned around, she picked up the book, and held it out to him. She suppressed a grin when he glanced over his shoulder to make sure none of his classmates had noticed his delay.

Timidly, with his gaze fixed on the novel, he approached the desk. He stopped a couple feet away, hooking his thumbs in his ill-fitting overall pockets, and peered at Lillian through blond bangs that hung at least a half inch below his eyebrows. "Ye mean, ye don't care if I take it home with me?"

"Not if it comes back with you on Monday."

His mouth quirked, and she could tell he was fighting a smile. According to a conversation she'd recently overheard between Brian and his peers, it wasn't popular for a thirteen-year-old boy to "cotton to book learnin'."

Brian reached for the book like it was a fragile treasure. "Thanks, Miss Gunter. I'll take real good care of it."

"I know you will." Before he could turn away, she added, "Another thing. You made an A on your history examination. I'm very proud of you."

A blush rushed to his freckled cheeks.

"You're a very bright young man. I hope you'll take advantage of your intelligence and obtain all the education you can."

A subtle light rose in his eyes. "Ye think I have enough intelligence to be a lawyer someday?"

A giddy thrill skipped across her chest. At least the boy was thinking about an education beyond the primitive grade school in Adela. "I think you're intelligent enough to be anything you want to be."

His sent her a sheepish grin, revealing a set of slightly crooked teeth, then shyly ducked his head.

"Why don't you run along now and catch up with your

friends?" she suggested.

With another "Thank ye, Miss Gunter," he headed for the door. When he was almost there, Lillian called his name again.

"I hope to see you at meeting on Sunday," she said.

He dropped his gaze a bit, breaking eye contact. "Maybe. . . if Daddy ain't workin'."

Lillian bristled. Most likely, his father would be recovering from a night and day with the bottle. Mr. Hawkins, like numerous miners in the area, often spent his meager wages carousing at the local saloon, leaving his family to scrape by on a pitiful little piece of earth he called a garden. Never mind that Brian needed a haircut and a new pair of overalls, or that his sister needed a new pair of shoes.

Lillian masked her indignation with a smile. "We'll pray that he isn't."

After Brian left, Lillian finished entering the grades in her notebook, then stored the school materials in the bottom of a storage closet near the entrance of the church. She then slid her Bible, a chapter of which she read to the class at the beginning of each day, and grade book into a leather satchel and wrapped a wool shawl around the shoulders of her plain, green dress.

She no longer bothered with dainty gloves and frilly parasols, embellishments that had been common accessories to her outing attire in Virginia. Instead, she'd toned down her entire wardrobe in order to blend in with the simpler style of the area women, the majority of whom were wives of struggling farmers or transient miners in search of an elusive mother lode.

When Lillian stepped out of the church, she turned toward the path that led along the Chestatee River. Uncle Frederick and Aunt Emma's house was a quarter of a mile from the church and one-half mile from the scant few buildings the area folks called "town," but Lillian didn't mind the walk. She found pleasure in strolling along the river, listening to the water dance over the rocks, and wandering through the patches of sunshine breaking through the trees.

She drew in a breath of crisp air that carried the faint scent of blooming wildflowers and budding trees. Somewhere nearby, a robin sang a *cheer-up* song, and a frisky titmouse answered with a melodious *teedle-dee, teedle-dee*. When she neared the bridge that spanned the river, the sounds of youthful laughter wafted through the air and mingled with the serene melodies of Mother Nature.

Lillian's steps slowed, and her bright spirit darkened. The Cherokee children lived within a stone's throw of the church where she taught school, yet they weren't allowed to attend because they were Indians—an atrocious injustice in Lillian's eyes. Why should they be denied an education because of their race? It wasn't fair.

She stopped at the mouth of the bridge, unconsciously raising her hand to the rough bark of an oak tree, and watched the children toss a ball back and forth with sticks that had some type of webbed net affixed to one end. There were four in all, ranging, Lillian guessed, from six to nine years of age.

Once, there had been several fine missionary schools for the Cherokee children, but those had rapidly dwindled amidst the conflict over the removal treaty. The children across the river were a few among many who no longer had access to English academics.

Lillian took a deep breath and released it slowly. She might not be able to change the law that banned the Indians from the white classroom, but she had been considering an idea that would give the children an equal opportunity to learn—if the Cherokee approved. She hadn't worked up the courage to approach them yet. With tensions running so high between the whites and the Cherokee right now, she didn't anticipate a warm reception.

A strand of hair that the wind had tugged free from her simple coiffure blew across her face. She tucked the errant lock behind her ear. The days were slipping by so fast. If she didn't make a move soon, and the removal did take place as predicted, she'd miss the opportunity to teach the children altogether.

Pulling back her shoulders in determination, she lifted the front of her skirt a few inches and ventured onto the bridge. When she was halfway across, a man stepped from behind a laurel thicket on the other side and blocked her path.

She stopped abruptly and took a startled step back. Her hand flew to her chest, where her heart beat like a captured wild bird's.

The stranger journeyed no further than his side of the bridge; but his stance—arms folded across his broad chest and his feet planted a little more than shoulder-width apart—clearly forbade her advance.

If the red turban he wore around the top of his head and the center-seam moccasins he wore on his feet were not enough to belie his ancestry, his shoulder-length, raven-black hair, light coppery complexion, and sharp, aristocratic features were. He was Cherokee, for sure; but not full-blood, for his eyes were as blue as the mist that hung over the distant mountain range behind him.

And menacing, like the sharpened edge of a silver blade.

A lump of fear rose in Lillian's throat. Who was he? What were his intentions? And why had he been hiding in the bushes, as though waiting for her?

She gauged the distance between her and the Indian, then forced her erratic heart to slow down. She had two strong legs and a healthy set of lungs. If he made one move toward her, surely she could run far enough and scream loud enough to attract the attention from someone in town.

She lowered her palm from her chest and clasped her hands in front of her. Swallowing, she wet her lips. "Hello. My name is Lillian Gunter. I'm the new schoolteacher in Adela. I was hoping I could speak with the parents of the children in your village about setting up a school for them."

"I know who you are and what you want. I'm afraid my people must decline your gracious offer."

His manner was civil, but his smooth, rich voice deadly calm.

A chill raced up her arms. "I see." Her rational mind told

her she should leave, but her instincts, like a finger to her back, pushed her forward, urging her to argue her case. "How many of the children are yours, Mister. . . ?"

"None. . .and all."

She had no idea what his answer meant and didn't feel inclined to ask. But she did feel a need to press her issue. "If I could just have a minute—"

"Haven't you heard, Miss Gunter? We will soon be forced to leave our nation and move west. Your lessons will do our children no good now."

"Do you honestly think President Van Buren will enforce that bogus treaty?" The "Phantom Treaty," as she had heard it called, had been signed in secret by twenty tribesmen without prior approval or knowledge of the Cherokee nation or its principal chief, John Ross. Even though it had been ratified almost two years ago, Lillian couldn't see how the United States government could justify enforcing such a fraudulent document.

"Yes, I do," he said, his voice ringing with a finality that fell between them like a death knell. "The Georgians will see to it."

Amidst the anger in his eyes, Lillian saw something else. A grief so deep, she felt the heavy hand of foreboding bearing down upon her own chest. "I'm sorry," she felt compelled to say. "I wish I could do something to help."

"You can. Stay on your side of the river. It's for your own good. . .as well as ours."

A befuddled frown pinched her forehead. "I don't understand."

"You will."

His steely gaze bored into hers, rendering her defenseless for a paralyzing moment. She couldn't breathe, couldn't speak. She wondered if she could even run if he took a threatening step toward her.

Then, without further comment or even a nod of dismissal, he turned and stalked away.

two

Still a bit awestruck by the Indian's overpowering presence, Lillian watched him retreat. The ends of his dark hair, glistening blue-black in the sun, wavered with each proud step he took toward the children. He held his broad shoulders erect, as though determined not to let the dark clouds looming over him and his people bend his fighting spirit.

As though he'd already forgotten his recent encounter with her, he joined the lively game with the children.

She pressed her hand against her stomach, where a peculiar fluttery sensation was just beginning to settle. While she had always had sympathy for the prospect of the Cherokee being forced from their land, she'd never really considered the impending removal "her" problem—something that would touch her life. Politics didn't interest her, nor did the details of the various treaties she often read about in the papers. Those resolutions, she figured, were better left up to the government and whatever other parties were involved.

But when she'd witnessed the desolation in the reticent Cherokee's eyes, his pain had touched her, and a fierce sense of conviction had swept through her. For the first time in her life, she felt inclined to catch the first stage to Washington and take on the "powers that be" herself.

The sound of footsteps falling on the bridge behind her penetrated her disconcerting thoughts. She spun around, releasing a relieved sigh when she found her cousin, Uncle Frederick and Aunt Emma's son, strolling toward her. "Thomas, you startled me."

The young attorney, who usually spent his days in his town office, stopped a couple feet away, swept back the sides of his dark suit coat, and slipped his hands into his pants pockets.

17

"I'm sorry. I didn't mean to."

"What brings you out this way?"

"I was out running an errand and decided to stop by and have lunch with you, Mother, and Father. Mother grew concerned when you didn't show up at your regular time, so I offered to come and look for you."

Lillian adjusted her satchel strap on her shoulder. "I'm sorry. I suppose I lingered longer than I intended to. I didn't mean to cause anyone any alarm, especially your mother."

He shrugged nonchalantly, holding on to his ever present smile that seemed to keep his eyes bright with amusement. "Don't worry about it. You know Mother. She wakes each morning fretting over whether or not the sun will rise."

Lillian's own lips tipped. "That's true. But, let's not give her another reason to worry. Let's go home, shall we?"

Knowing Thomas wasn't a lover of nature, Lillian didn't suggest they continue along the river path. Instead, she trudged up the jutted side road leading from the bridge to the main road, which provided a more civilized path to her aunt's house. Thomas fell into step beside her.

As they strolled along in silence, Lillian's thoughts returned to her recent meeting with the Indian. When she told him she wished she could do something to help, he'd told her to stay on her side of the river. Her lips thinned in ire. She wanted to do more than stay on her side of the river. She wanted to send a letter to the governor, address Congress, and argue the Cherokees' case before the president.

Frustration joined the anger building in her chest. Even if all those feats were within her grasp, she knew they'd do little good. Who was going to listen to her? She was a woman. She couldn't even vote.

"Lillian," Thomas said from somewhere behind her. "Do you mind slowing down a bit?"

She stopped and waited for him to catch up.

"You were charging the air like an angry bull," he said when their shoulders were once again abreast. "What's gotten you so worked up?"

She didn't mind telling him, but not while she was so "worked up," as he had put it. She feared she'd sound like a blithering idiot, not a disciplined teacher of children. Searching her mind for another excuse, she settled on Brian and his ill-fitting overalls. "I was just thinking about one of my students. He needs new clothes, but his father spends all his earnings on the bottle."

Thomas folded his hands behind his back. "That's a shame."

"Yes. It is." Turning her thoughts to Brian only increased her frustration. She struggled against the urge to walk faster.

"Lillian, may I ask you something?"

"Of course."

He stopped, prompting her to do the same. When she turned to face him, he was no longer smiling.

"What were you doing on the bridge?" he asked.

"I had hoped to speak with the Cherokee parents about teaching their children."

"Lillian, you know Indian children aren't allowed in our schools." He sounded like he was chiding a child about to break a well-known rule.

"I know that," she returned flatly. "I was thinking of holding class in one of their homes during the afternoon hours."

"I don't think that would be wise."

"Neither did the man who stopped me."

Thomas's brow dipped in confusion.

"The gentleman playing with the children," she explained. "He blocked my way when I started to cross the bridge."

Thomas's frown melted into a knowing grin. "So you met our industrious miller, Ethan Walker."

She arched her brows. "Oh, is that his name?"

"I take it he didn't introduce himself."

Taking the initiative, she commenced walking. "Not hardly. In fact, he was rather aloof."

Her cousin hunched his shoulders in a seemingly nonchalant gesture. "Ethan's all right. He just doesn't have a lot to say, and he has a lot on his mind lately."

"The removal?"

"Yes."

Lillian tipped her head and looked up at Thomas. Once again, his expression was grim, which didn't surprise her. She gathered through a few offhand comments he'd made that his sympathies lay with the Cherokee, also.

"Isn't there something someone can do to stop it?" she asked.

He released a forlorn sigh. "Those of us who care have tried. I, myself, have written numerous letters to various governmental delegates. Father and I spoke with the governor last year on the Cherokees' behalf. We even tried to secure an appointment with Congress, but all of our pleas seem to fall on deaf ears."

So that was it. The Cherokees' fate was sealed. A bleak wave of sorrow swept through her, and a pair of desolate, blue eyes surfaced in her mind.

Simultaneously, she and Thomas stepped onto the front lawn of Aunt Emma and Uncle Frederick's modest, white-washed house. The smell of pot roast and corn bread drifted on the air, but Lillian hadn't yet worked up an appetite. "The removal is still two months away," she said. "What would be wrong with me teaching the Indian children until then?"

"There's too much conflict between the Georgia landowners and the Cherokee right now. You don't want to get caught in the middle of that."

Lillian didn't fancy anyone telling her what she did or did not want to do. She'd long ago surmised that if God had not wanted her to figure out her desires for herself, He would not have given her the ability to think. Lifting her dress a few inches, she climbed the front steps. "But I'm not a Georgia landowner. The battle between them and the Cherokee has nothing to do with me."

"It will if you try to teach the Indian children."

His voice held an underlying note of warning. She stopped beside him in front of the door and turned to study his usually pleasant features. His expression held no warmth or affability. Just solemn seriousness.

"Thomas, I came here to teach the children of Adela," she said, "and that's exactly what I intend to do. But that doesn't mean the townspeople own me. As long as I do nothing to blemish my reputation or discredit my credentials as a teacher, they can't dictate what I do in my own time."

"Things are a lot different here than they are at your home in Virginia, Lillian. *Please,* take my advice, as well as Ethan's. Don't get involved." His features softened, his eyes warmed with concern. "Trust me, my dear cousin. It's for your own good." Ever the gentleman, he pushed open the door and stepped back, motioning her to enter ahead of him.

She stepped across the threshold considering what he had told her. She'd received the same warning from two different men in the same day. She wasn't sure what to make of it, or what, exactly, she was going to do about it.

After all, she never had been one to heed warnings.

❧

Lillian stood with her arms crossed, staring out her open bedroom window at the veiled shadows of trees mottled with silvery streaks of moonlight. Restless katydids ground out a shrill and steady song, and every once in a while, a lone owl released a low and eerie *hoo-hoo*. In the distance, the gurgling waters of the Chestatee droned out its own hypnotic tune.

Everyone else had retired over an hour ago, but she was too befuddled to sleep. Should she do as Thomas and the Indian had said and stay away from the Cherokee children? Or should she do what her heart was telling her to do and find a way to teach them?

Releasing a despondent sigh, she leaned her shoulder against the window frame. She wasn't all that concerned about herself. If she did manage to set up lessons for the children, she might receive a few complaints, or even be asked to stop—nothing she couldn't handle.

But what about the Indians? Would someone vent his or her grievances on them because of something she alone was responsible for? The last thing she wanted to do was cause them more adversity. They had enough of that to contend with in light of the upcoming removal.

She gazed up at the full moon nestled in a star-spangled blanket of black velvet. Why was the plight of the Cherokee bothering her so? She'd never felt so impassioned about anything in her life. But, then, she'd never looked into the eyes of a man like Ethan Walker and seen such desperation. . .or such ancestral pride. He was proud of who he was, in spite of the blatant scorn of the ignorant.

She closed her eyes and gave her head a clearing shake. Why was she thinking so much about Ethan? Not only now, but the entire afternoon. *He* wasn't the target of her concern. It was the entire Cherokee nation.

And the children, who had no one to teach them.

A whimsical breeze ruffled her drawn-back curtains and fluttered through her hair, awakening her sense of adventure. She turned from the window and scanned the four, small walls of her bedroom, shimmering like rippling water in a solitary candle's light. Suddenly, she felt confined. Tonight, she needed to do more than breathe the fresh air through her open window. She needed to feel the dew on her skin, walk beneath a blanket of stars, and embrace the freedom of the vast openness.

Having already taken down her hair, she considered tying her heavy mane back with a ribbon, then decided against it. Who was going to see her anyway—besides the owls and the katydids?

She grabbed her dark cloak from a peg near the door and blew out the candle on her dresser. Quietly, she slipped from her room and worked her way through the dark house, making her escape through the back door.

She had often taken late-night walks on the plantation. Communing with God and nature had sometimes been her only solace during her mother's illness and after her unexpected breakup with James. Now, she needed that solace again. She needed to find that quiet place inside her so she could hear that still, small voice when God spoke to her and told her what she should do about teaching the Cherokee children.

Trapped in her own deep thoughts, she strolled along her favorite path beside the river until she almost reached the bridge, then something that didn't quite fit in with the night sounds captured her attention. Stopping, she listened. Sure enough, the wind carried the whistled tune of an old hymn she had heard recently.

Befuddlement pinched her brow. Who could it be? Would Ethan Walker be lingering around the bridge this time of night? As quickly as the thought evolved, she shook her head in denial. She couldn't see the reserved Indian whistling a tune, especially a religious one.

Gingerly, she crept forward until she could see the bridge. There she found the source of the divine melody in the form of a man crossing from the other side. When he stepped from the shadows into the moonlight, Lillian drew back in surprise, almost gasping aloud.

It was almost midnight. She thought everyone else was at home in bed, but she'd been wrong.

What had Uncle Frederick been doing across the river?

❧

She'd seen her uncle. Now she would start asking questions, poking her nose into business where it didn't belong.

Ethan receded into the shadow of the large oak tree where he was hiding. A while ago, when he'd caught a glimpse of something moving along the riverbank, he'd come to make sure a member of the malicious pony clubs wasn't lying in wait for the unsuspecting preacher. But the glint he'd seen had not been the metal of a gun or knife blade; it'd been the moonlight reflecting off Lillian Gunter's pale hair, like gold dust in the sun.

Between his thumb and forefinger, he rolled a small, smooth pebble he'd picked up when he'd climbed the riverbank. What was the crazy white woman doing outside after dark? Why wasn't she at home in bed, where she belonged?

He heard the rustle of dried pine needles beneath her feet

when she turned. She'd walked right past him a few minutes ago, totally unaware of his presence. And she would again. If he were a deviant, he could have her on the ground and be taking advantage of her before she realized what was happening to her.

A swift and unexpected sense of protection clutched Ethan's chest. Out wandering through the woods at night, she was asking for trouble. Someone needed to teach her a lesson, and it looked like he was the chosen one.

He peeked around the lower side of the tree and tossed the pebble he was holding so it landed unobtrusively on the path behind her. She spun around, presenting her back to him, and searched the shadows around her.

Ethan slipped from his hiding place and eased up behind her.

"Who's there?" she ventured in a small, childlike voice.

He felt her fear. Smelled it. Tasted it. Satisfaction and guilt warred within him. The guilt he swept aside, reminding himself his efforts were for her own good.

He stopped with only two feet between them. Her hair cascaded down her back like a shimmering waterfall, begging for his touch. But he refused to let the long, silken strands divert his attention from his purpose, resisted the allure of her sweet, lavender scent.

As anticipated, she turned in haste and slammed into him. He snapped his left arm around her, deftly trapping her arms at her sides, and clamped his right hand over her mouth.

For one so small, she put up an impressive fight, like a wildcat backed into a corner. After a few intense seconds, the feel of her shapely body struggling against him cracked his reserve. The swell of hysteria rising from her throat pricked a layer of his conscience. He supposed he'd put enough fear in her to keep her indoors after dark.

"Take it easy, Miss Gunter," he murmured, keeping his voice low so her uncle wouldn't hear from the road. "I'm not going to harm you."

Like a leaf falling into a dead wind, she stopped struggling. The moonlight shining through a clearing in the trees granted him a lucid view of her face. Her forest green eyes widened in surprise, then narrowed in anger. Like a winded lioness, her chest started heaving. A few degrees more, and the air spewing from her nostrils would have burned him.

A grin of admiration tugged at the corners of Ethan's mouth. He'd never seen such tumultuous fury and exquisite beauty at the same time and on the same face. Her volatile loveliness tempted a need deep inside him, a need that had not been satisfied for a very long time. He tempered his desire. Now was not the time to entertain thoughts of kissing a woman—especially a white one.

"If I take my hand away, are you going to scream?" he asked. Something equally unsettling occurred to him. Something she, at the moment, was quite capable of. "Or bite me?"

She neither shook her head nor nodded, just continued glaring up at him like he'd just slung mud on her best dress.

"I said, 'are you going to scream?' "

Nothing changed in her stormy demeanor, and he couldn't help but admire her stubborn staying power.

"All right, Miss Gunter, this is what I'm going to do. I'm going to remove my hand, and if you make one sound, even a small one, that might attract someone's attention, I will pick you up and carry you all the way back to your uncle's house with my hand clamped over your mouth. And I assure you, the journey will not be a pleasant one."

Keeping his left arm secure around her, he cautiously eased his right hand away from her mouth. When he was certain she wasn't going to scream, he let his palm rest on the nearest logical place—her shoulder.

"Take. . .your. . .hands. . .off. . .me," she hissed through clenched teeth.

He heard it in the disdain in her voice, saw it in the fiery darts shooting from her eyes. The word "savage" was so clearly embedded in her mind, it could have been engraved on her forehead. A searing arrow of rage shot through him. He released her so abruptly, she stumbled backward. When she fell, landing on her backside, he fought the instinctive urge to reach for her.

She braced herself with her palms on the ground, a few inches behind her hips, and glowered up at him. "You despicable man."

Her blatant description of him almost took him aback. "Savage" he knew how to deal with, from experience. But he'd never been called despicable before. He felt she thought him vile instead of barbaric.

He preferred barbaric.

Swiftly, he changed the direction of his thoughts. What did he care what she thought of him? She wasn't a person of consequence to his life. Never would be.

Deciding his next practical move was to get her home, he reached down his hand to her. She ignored his gesture, scrambling up on her own, which didn't surprise him. He dropped his hand back to his side.

Looking down, she adjusted her cloak. The visible trembling in her hands betrayed how shaken she still was.

Ethan's emotions weighed equally between irritation and regret. Didn't she realize if he meant her any harm, the deed would be done by now? "What do you think I'm going to do, Miss Gunter? Scalp you? Hang my bounty out in the sun to dry?"

Her head snapped up. Her green eyes flashed with rekindled fury. "First, you hide behind the thicket at the bridge and jump out at me."

He had not *jumped* out at her, but he figured it'd do little good to point that out to her in her present state of mind.

She curled her fists at her sides like she was about to charge him. "Then, you sneak up behind me in the dark. You tell me; what am I supposed to think?"

"I assure you, my intentions were honorable."

She arched her elegant winged eyebrows. "Oh? You have a strange way of showing it."

She straightened her spine, looking very much like the no-nonsense teacher he envisioned her to be—except for all that pale hair spilling over her shoulders. That enticing feature reminded him of a moon princess.

"Now," she said, "if you will kindly step aside, I'd like to go home."

"I'll walk with you."

"That isn't necessary."

"Maybe not, but I'll walk with you anyway."

Her lips curled into a thin line. "Mr. Walker, this is ridiculous—"

His temper flared. Her willful independence would surely be the death of her. . .or him. "No. What's ridiculous is you traipsing through the woods at night, alone." He somehow managed to keep his voice low.

She lifted her chin a defiant inch. "And what concern is that of yours?"

"None," he said, and told himself he meant it. "But I happen to think highly of your aunt and uncle. . .and your cousin. If I were to allow you to walk yourself home and something happened to you, I'd never be able to look them in the eye again."

She didn't have an immediate response. He could see her struggling with her decision, which, even though she probably didn't want to admit it, he had already made for her.

Her breathing intensified. Her chest rose and fell in renewed indignation. He sensed her coming to the realization that she had two choices: to make her journey home hard, or easy.

"Fine," she quipped. "Walk me home, but don't expect a pleasant conversationalist."

He really wasn't sure why he found her feisty petulance so amusing. . .and attractive. But he did and decided to make the best of it. He quirked a taunting brow. "Now, why on earth would I expect you to disappoint me?"

The delicate muscle in her jaw tensed. Rancor flashed in her eyes. Good thing those eyes weren't sharp. If they were, he'd certainly be headless by now. Stepping to the side, he said, "May we go?" Then he presented his arm to her, just to see what she would do.

Lifting the front of her dress a few inches, she blew past him like a snowflake in a blizzard. As he turned to follow, he caught a glimpse of the shiny leaves of a low-lying laurel branch that had snaked across the trail directly in her path.

"Watch the—"

Her booted foot snagged the branch, propelling her forward. Her flailing arms flew up to do battle with the ground.

Ethan launched forward, reaching for her and grabbing nothing but air. He grimaced as her body slapped the earth with a blunt thud. A hearty "Oooof" shot from her lungs, and her pale tresses fanned out around her head like the tail feathers of a cocky gobbler.

"Limb," he said, sheepishly finishing his warning.

With a sense of dread, he ventured forward, toward the top of her head. This was all he needed, a wildcat with a sore tail and an aching stomach. She was sure to come up scratching.

three

The fall knocked the rage out of Lillian, leaving behind a sense of humiliation as distasteful as the dirt in her mouth. Had she not allowed her anger to take control of her actions, she would not have stomped past the Indian like a "charging bull," as Thomas had put it earlier that afternoon. And, most likely, she would have seen the offensive object she'd tripped over.

Spitting, she managed to rid her mouth of a pine needle and a considerable amount of grit. She wanted to get up, but at the moment, she couldn't move. Her stomach felt like a huge tree had fallen on it.

Something brushed her cheek, but she was too stunned to react, except to turn her head to see what kind of creature was about to devour her. To her relief, she found Ethan Walker had swept back her curtain of hair and was peering down at her from a kneeling position.

"Are you all right?" he asked.

She nodded, once.

"Would you like for me to help you up?"

She swallowed, hard, and found that pride did not go down so easily. "Please," she rasped, for the fall had taken her wind.

Hooking an arm around her waist, he lifted her like she was a sack of feathers and held on to her until she was steady on her feet.

He had to be at least six-foot-two, a good head and neck taller than she. He could have crushed her with one hand, if he'd wanted to. But he hadn't, and he wouldn't. At least, she didn't think he would. Somehow, she sensed all he wanted to do was frighten her, and he had surely succeeded.

Intending to delay looking at him until she regained some of her dignity, she glanced down and started to brush off her cloak. When her smarting hands came in contact with the rough wool, she winced.

She watched as two larger hands, a few shades darker than hers, even in the moonlight, reached out and captured her wrists. His calloused touch was amazingly gentle. . .and strangely unsettling. She lifted her gaze to his face and found his expression full of concern. His dark hair, now free of the turban but pulled back to his nape and tied with a thin leather strap, glistened like black satin in the moon's glow.

"Your hands are cut," he said. "They need cleaning." Like an eagle swooping down for its prey, he bent and scooped her up into the cradle of his arms.

Startled, she hooked her arms around his neck. "Mr. Walker, what are you doing?"

"We need water. The river's the closest source." Turning, he trudged toward the riverbank.

"I can walk."

"You may fall again."

"Suppose you fall. Then we'll both go down."

He paused at the top of the hill and gazed down at her, his expression hidden in the shadowed planes of his face. "I won't," he said, his velvet-edged voice stoic and low.

Was that Arrogance speaking? Or Confidence?

When he loped down the bank with the agility of a roe, his sinewy stomach muscles rippling against her hip, she decided it was Confidence. But, good heavens! What had she expected?

He plunked her down on a large, smooth rock. Pulling a handkerchief from his back pocket, he crouched with his back to her and dipped the cloth into the water.

Moonlight danced on the currents like sunlight on beveled glass. A lamenting whippoorwill had awakened and joined in the song of the burbling river and piping katydids.

Fleetingly, the thought crossed her mind that she should be arguing with him, demanding he see her home immediately. After all, the man had scared her senseless a few minutes ago. . .and humiliated her as no one else ever had—except

James, her former fiancé.

But she didn't argue. Instead, she just sat there, like an injured child, waiting for him to cleanse her wounds.

She looked down at the scrapes on her hands. One could hardly call them wounds. They were little more than surface scratches that had secreted a drop or two of blood. Yet she had winced openly when she started to brush off her cloak. He must think her weak and fragile, a whining tenderfoot.

Lifting her gaze, she focused on the broad back of the man wringing water from his handkerchief and her brow dipped in consternation. She shouldn't care what he thought about her. Yet she did. Befuddlement drifted into her mind. For some reason that she couldn't put her finger on, she cared considerably what this reserved Cherokee thought of her.

He turned in his kneeling position, and when he met her gaze, he froze. "What's wrong?"

"Nothing," she replied a bit too quickly. "Why?"

"You look like you're in pain."

Realizing she was still frowning, she forced her brow to smooth. "I'm fine. I was just thinking."

He studied her a moment. "I see," he finally said, and picked up her hand.

Inwardly, she breathed a sigh of relief. Thank goodness he hadn't asked her *what* she was thinking about. If he had, she would have had to come up with something fictitious, because she certainly couldn't tell him that he was the object of her perplexing thoughts.

He cradled her hand in warmth while he bathed each palm in coolness. After he finished with her hands, he twisted around and wet the handkerchief again. When he turned back to her, he raised a hand toward her face. Caught off guard by his unexpected action, she flinched.

His hand froze a few inches from her chin. On the side of his face illuminated by the moon, his jaw muscle flexed. He withdrew his hand and propped his forearm on his raised knee. "I'm not going to hurt you, Miss Gunter," he said, his voice ringing with chafe. "I had hoped you would have figured that out by now."

"I know. You just took me by surprise when you raised your hand."

A deep frown marred his forehead. "Has someone raised their hand to you before?"

Was that anger she now heard in his voice? "No," she told him. "Of course not."

A brief silence full of volatile energy passed. "I see," the Indian said, his tone now possessing a steel edge.

She knew what he was thinking. That she was afraid of him because of his race. That she was judgmental and prejudiced like those pushing for the removal. Her recently tempered anger stirred. She met his gaze with challenge. "My response wasn't directed at you personally, Mr. Walker. If I were afraid of you, do you think I'd be sitting here allowing you to wash my hands without offering some sort of resistance?"

Gradually, the muscle in his jaw relaxed. Holding her gaze, as though to gauge her reaction, he raised his hand again and captured her chin between his thumb and forefinger.

A flutter of alarm stirred in her chest. Or was it something else? She felt no instinctive need to get up and flee. Yet his touch had, for some reason, kicked up a lively dance inside her chest.

Tipping her face toward the moonlight, he started cleansing a spot on her left lower lip with the freshly dampened cloth. "You have a small cut on your lip," he said. "Nothing to be alarmed about. It won't even leave a scar. But it will be sore for a few days, as will your hands. I'm sure your aunt will have some salve that will take the sting out."

The moist handkerchief felt like the feather of a baby bird's wing whispering against her mouth. His hand supported her chin like a soft down pillow. How could it be that the hands that had held her so roughly a short while ago now touched her with such tenderness? She swallowed and, without thinking, flicked out the tip of her tongue to wet her lips.

Ethan froze with the cloth hovering close to her mouth, his

gaze snapping up to hers. For a split instant, the entire world, even the flowing waters of the Chestatee, stopped moving. A thousand tiny butterflies took flight in Lillian's stomach, then rose to thrash against her ribs. Her lungs, it seemed, couldn't get enough air.

Then Ethan blinked, and the magical moment was gone.

Brow wrinkled in concentration, he focused back on her mouth and continued his adept ministrations.

Lillian drew in a deep, calming breath. What was wrong with her? What was invoking all these strange, new feelings?

Ethan Walker.

The name drifted through her mind like a soft summer breeze. She closed her eyes, trying to block out his handsome face, just a breath away from hers. He couldn't be the source of her whimsical reactions. She hardly knew the man.

But her fickle emotions battled back. She had been engaged for two years to one of the most handsome men in Wilmington. Yet, James's touch had never made her feel so alive. . .or flustered. . .or left her feeling chilled when he took his hand away—like Ethan's did.

Slowly, she opened her eyes, and found herself looking directly into his face. Like stardust descending from heaven, the magic returned. For a breathless space in time, his hooded gaze bore into hers, bypassing her defenseless façade and reaching to her soul. Then his gaze dropped to her mouth.

The sudden awareness of what was about to happen took her breath away. Heaven help her, he was going to kiss her, and she didn't know if she could stop him. But what she found even more frightening was that she didn't know if she wanted to.

Like a startled buck changing directions, Ethan stood. "I think it's time I got you home, Miss Gunter."

Once again, a chill swept over her. She shuddered in spite of the heavy cloak draped around her shoulders. Carefully moderating her voice, hoping to keep it steady, she said, "I think, Mr. Walker, you are probably right."

He tucked his wet handkerchief in his belt and scooped her

up into his arms.

"Really, Mr. Walker, I can walk. There's nothing wrong with my legs."

"When we get up the bank," came his blunt response. Without pause, he took his first step.

Left with no other choice, she slipped her arms around his neck and braced for the trek. He carried her up the embankment with as much deftness as he had carried her down. When they reached the top, he set her on her feet as promised. To her surprise, she found her legs a bit shaky, but not so unsteady she couldn't make it home—as long as another inconspicuous object didn't lay in her path.

With a daring degree of challenge in his veiled expression, he offered her his arm.

Irritation pressed her lips together in a thin line. *Stubborn Cherokee.* He was determined to prove her a bigot. She straightened her spine. She was equally determined to prove him wrong. Offering him an amicable smile, she slipped her hand through the crook of his elbow, refusing to wince when contact with the smooth material of his homespun shirt aggravated her scraped palm.

"Do your hands still hurt?" he asked, as though reading her mind.

A little, but he'd never know that. "They're fine. Shall we go?"

Together, they set out at a casual pace.

A dozen puzzling questions circled her mind, the first being: What was Uncle Frederick doing across the river in the middle of the night? Since she could go straight to the source for the answer to that inquiry, she skipped to the next question plaguing her mind.

"Mr. Walker, you insist that I stay on *my* side of the river, yet you don't hesitate to come over here. Why is that?"

"Tonight, you were the reason I crossed."

A lot that told her. He obviously wasn't going to volunteer any information. "And why is that?"

"When I saw movement along the riverbank, I thought you might be a member of the pony clubs."

"Pony clubs?"

"They're vigilantes, Miss Gunter, outlaws who profit by robbing and terrorizing my people."

A flicker of trepidation coursed through her. She obviously had no idea what the Indians had endured over the past few years. . .or decades. "So you came to investigate?" she prompted further.

"That's right."

"Why didn't you just leave when you saw it was me?"

He didn't answer.

"I wasn't on *your* side of the river."

Still, he said nothing.

She resisted the urge to look heavenward and shake her head. She might as well be talking to the moon.

Tilting her head, she looked up at him, silently willing him to return her gaze. He didn't, although she was certain he was aware of her attention. When he passed from shadow to a patch of moonlight, she noted his expression was stoic.

His lack of response riled her all over again. He had taken at least ten years off her life when he had sneaked up behind her on the path earlier, and she deserved to know why. "Do I look like a member of the pony clubs, Mr. Walker?" she asked, not attempting to hide her agitation. "Is that why you found it necessary to frighten me half to death?"

Before she knew what was happening, he stopped, whipped her around, and captured her upper arms, pulling her against his solid body. Somehow, her palms ended up flat against his sinewy chest, where his heart drummed like a wild horse stampede.

"I did it, Miss Gunter, to prove a point."

The harshness in his tone sent a chill racing down her spine. His warm breath raked her face like the wind preceding a summer storm. A quick and sudden panic leapt to her throat, threatening to choke her. Her confidence that she was safe with him trembled.

Then she reminded herself who he was: her aunt and uncle's friend. They had both spoken highly of Ethan Walker and his family when Lillian had mentioned meeting him. Thomas had also used kind words to describe him. And Uncle Frederick had visited the man's homestead in the middle of the night.

She may know little about Ethan Walker, but she knew her relatives well. They would not think favorably of someone capable of delivering unprovoked violence.

Swallowing her fear, she met his incensed expression with staunch determination. "And what point were you trying to prove, Mr. Walker?"

His grip on her arms tightened, stopping short of pain. He dipped his head closer, until they were practically nose to nose. "The pony clubs may be targeting my people, but let me assure you, if one, or more, of them saw a woman like you out tramping through the woods at night, the results would be tragic."

Her eyes stretched wide in shock. Her mouth dropped open in ire. " 'A woman like *me?* Tramping through the *woods?*' What is *that* supposed to mean?"

"It means, Miss Gunter, that you are too beautiful. . .*and* too tempting, for a man with a depraved mind to resist."

She blinked. Had he just said she was beautiful. . .and tempting? Even James had never told her that she was tempting. Should she feel complemented. . .or offended? She opened her mouth to respond, but the entire English language failed her.

Gradually, he released his grasp on her arms and stepped back.

Her palms floated away from his chest. With her hands suddenly feeling empty, she clasped them in front of her. After drawing in two breaths that belonged to her alone, she regained a small degree of rationality. "So what you're saying is that you wanted to show me just how easily I could be attacked."

"And raped."

She glanced away, deep in thought.

❧

Ethan could see she was uncomfortable with his bold use of language. He could have used a milder word, but she was turning out to be harder to convince than he'd anticipated. She needed to see how much danger her late-night escapade had put her in. If uncensored language helped him accomplish that feat, then so be it. "Miss Gunter, I assume you were allowed to come and go pretty much as you pleased at your plantation home in Virginia."

She swiveled her head back around and looked up at him, her green eyes full of question. "You know where I'm from?"

"Your aunt and uncle mentioned it to me."

"I see." She studied him a contemplative moment. "You're right. I did have liberty to go anywhere on the plantation grounds without fearing for my safety."

"Things are very different here."

"That's what Thomas said."

"Well, you should listen to your cousin."

The corners of her mouth eased up in a conceding smile, spawning a warm glow in her eyes. "He said the same thing about you."

That revelation surprised Ethan. Still, he found himself smiling in response to Lillian's amicable expression. "Well, then, how can you argue with that?"

She glanced away, staring across her right shoulder, apparently weighing out her next words. As she contemplated, the tip of her pink tongue flicked out and curled over her lower lip.

A spark of longing coiled inside Ethan. In all of his twenty-six years, he had never been so aware of a woman's every little move. Apparently without realizing it, she played an alluring game of seduction. He folded his hands behind his back and waited. When she looked back at him, he forced himself to focus on her eyes and not on her wet mouth.

"Are the pony clubs the reason you don't want me teaching the Cherokee children?" she wanted to know.

"Yes. That and the present animosity between my people and yours."

"*My* people? *Yours?* You make it sound as though I support the removal."

He quirked an inquisitive brow. "Do you?"

Her eyes snapped hot with wrath. "Of course not! It's the most despicable thing I've ever heard of."

Her fighting spirit was back, only this time, her hostility wasn't aimed at him. A thread of amusement wove through him, along with an even larger strand of respect. An easy grin pulled at the corner of his mouth. "Oh? I was under the impression that I was."

Her brow wrinkled in befuddlement for a few thoughtful seconds, then smoothed in realization. "Yes, um, well. I apologize for calling you despicable, Mr. Walker. I was angry."

"I know."

She lifted her chin an obstinate inch. "I won't apologize for being angry. I had a right."

He noted the stubborn set of her lips and the unbending glint in her eyes that dared him to disagree, and smiled. "Yes, you did."

She studied him another scrutinizing moment, as though trying to figure out whether or not he was serious, then turned and commenced walking. When he fell into step beside her, she slipped her hand back into the crook of his arm—to Ethan, a mild and pleasant surprise.

"Miss Gunter?" he said after they had traveled a few quiet steps.

"Yes, Mr. Walker."

"Are you going to venture out anymore after dark?"

She didn't answer right away, and Ethan began to fear his efforts had been in vain.

"I suppose not," she finally said. "At least, not without an escort."

The last she added like an afterthought, like she was determined not to give him the satisfaction of having the final say in her nightly goings and comings.

He looked down at her, appreciating her striking profile. "Good. I'll not apologize for scaring you half to death, then."

A tiny smile lifted the corner of her mouth.

He stopped in an area shrouded by shadows, just short of stepping into Frederick's moonlit yard, and turned to her. "I'll wait here until you're safely inside."

Without moonlight raining down on her lovely face, he couldn't read her expression, but he sensed her hesitation. "You'll be safe from here," he assured her. "I promise."

"It's not that."

"Oh?"

At least three pensive seconds passed. "Is there a reason my relatives shouldn't see us together?"

No, there wasn't. He trusted her aunt and uncle completely. But he wasn't certain someone else wasn't watching from a distance. He didn't see a benefit in telling Lillian that, though. "At this time of night, I don't think your relatives would appreciate seeing you alone with any man."

She sweetened the air with a resigned sigh. "You're probably right."

He knew he should send her on her way, but his instincts told him she wanted to linger. Apparently, her inquisitive mind wasn't satisfied.

"Mr. Walker—"

"You know," he interrupted, "I would rather you call me Ethan."

A silence filled with wavering followed.

He knew that in her world, first names came with time and familiarity. Perhaps she was right to hesitate. Perhaps he had been wrong in suggesting she call him Ethan. After all, theirs was a relationship destined to go no further.

"All right, then," she said, giving pause to his thoughts of retracting his request. "You may call me Lillian."

"Lillian," he repeated in little more than a murmur. He liked the sound and feel of her name rolling off his tongue. "Lovely," he added.

"Thank you, Mister. . .*Ethan*."

He liked the way she said his name, too. All refined and proper. No one had ever said it quite that way before.

"As I started to say," she went on, "would the Cherokee children really be in danger if I taught them?"

"Yes. And so would you."

The rhythmic cry of the whippoorwill, the piercing shrill of the katydids, and the gentle murmur of the river were the only sounds that filled the next quarter minute.

"I understand," Lillian finally said, her voice heavy with disappointment.

Ethan thought he understood. She was laying down her weapons before the battle began, not because she wanted to, but because she had just realized the enemy was too strong. Defeat, Ethan knew, was not a pleasant companion.

"I would never do anything to bring harm to the children," she added. "I'll not mention teaching them again." She started to go.

Instinctively, he reached for her hand. When she turned back to him, he said, "Lillian, I regret that things are as they are." More than she knew. "And I appreciate your concern. But there's nothing you can do right now for the children. The circumstances are beyond our control."

"I know," she whispered, and closed her small hand firmly around his.

A bleak and forlorn silence full of lost hope and unfulfilled dreams passed between them. Standing there in the dark, holding her dainty hand in his, he caught a glimpse of her soul. She was not biased. She accepted him and his people for who and what they were, without prejudice or reservation. He almost wished she didn't. Then he could walk away and easily put her out of his mind.

"Ethan," she said, her mellow voice elbowing into his pensive thoughts. "I've never gone to sleep hungry or awakened wondering where my next meal would come from. I've never had to watch a loved one suffer at the hands of another. I've never had to worry over where I would live in two months. . . or even two years."

Ethan realized that Lillian was apologizing for leading a privileged life. Her humble profession gave him an even clearer picture of who she was. A woman who followed her heart, a path that could lead to both rewards. . .and danger.

"I can't even begin to imagine how you and your people

must feel," she finished.

"And I hope you never do," he said, and meant it.

"I am *so* sorry. If it were in my power to purchase this land, I would gladly give it back to you."

He heard a catch in her voice, and for the first time in his life, he followed his own heart and pulled her into his arms. When he felt her slip her arms around him, his chest swelled with an unfamiliar emotion. He cradled the back of her head with his hand. "You have no reason to be sorry, *aquatseli Liliyani.*"

"Aqua-what?"

He smiled. "*Aquatseli Liliyani.* It's 'Lillian' in Cherokee." Actually, it was "*my* Lillian." But he couldn't tell her that. He could never let her know she had, this night, touched a lasting place in his heart.

"How do you say 'Ethan' in Cherokee?"

"*Itana.*"

"*Itana,*" she repeated softly.

The sound of his name flowing from her lips in his native tongue unleashed emotions Ethan never knew existed. An amorous shudder rolled through him, rocking him to the center of his being. He angled his head and inhaled her sweet lavender fragrance, and the more heady scent that was her own. He let his hand glide down the silken smoothness of her thick, pale hair.

Warmth curled in his stomach and a deeper need rose within his breast. His throat ached to taste the sweetness of her lips. His heart longed to sate the desire growing inside him. She reminded him he was flesh and blood, made him feel alive—something he hadn't felt for a very long time.

But the blood running through his veins was Cherokee, and the bridge that spanned the differences in their worlds was much too wide to cross. It would be foolish to even take the first step.

His last thought gave him the strength to slide his hands to her upper arms and gently set her away from him. But the feel of her soft, warm body in his arms lingered, branding him with a memory that he knew would stay with him for many nights to come.

"You should go in now," Ethan said. "Before someone misses you."

Slowly, reluctantly, it seemed, her arms fell away from his waist. "You're right. I should. Good night, Ethan. Thank you for seeing me home."

"It was my pleasure."

He watched her cross the moonlit yard. When she reached the door, she stopped and looked back, offering one last wave to the shadows where he stood. He waited until she stepped inside and closed the door.

"Good-bye, my *Liliyani*," he whispered, then turned and quietly slipped away.

four

"Lillian?"

Lillian turned from closing the door. "Hello, Uncle Frederick." The pleasant smell of boiling coffee wafted from the kitchen fireplace.

From outside, she had seen the glow of candlelight through the parlor window and figured her uncle was still up. Apparently, he'd heard her slipping in the back door and had come to investigate.

Balancing the candleholder in one hand, he stepped further into the kitchen. Tall and lanky, the middle-aged preacher seemed to swallow up half the room. "Where on earth have you been?" he asked.

She reached up and unfastened the cloak button at her throat. "I couldn't sleep, so I went for a walk."

"Alone?"

Should she tell her uncle she had literally run into Ethan? She didn't like the idea of lying, even if the untruth was one of omission. On the other hand, Ethan had said her relatives would not appreciate her being alone with any man so late at night. Why cause unnecessary concern? "Yes, Uncle Frederick. I went alone."

Frederick stepped closer, his heavy, graying eyebrows drawn together in concern. "Lillian, you shouldn't be out after dark by yourself."

She really didn't want to get into a discussion with Uncle Frederick over her late-night walk. The debate she'd had with Ethan had been plenty enough. "I know. I tripped over something in my path and took a spill. That was enough to convince me I should stay indoors after dark." She hoped her explanation was reasonable enough to satisfy her uncle.

"Did you get hurt?"

"Just a small cut on my lip and some scrapes on my hands. Nothing to worry about."

He held the candle up to her face and studied her mouth. "It looks like it's already been cleaned."

Oh, dear. Now what did she tell him? "Yes," she said straightaway to avoid hesitation that might make her uncle suspicious. To her dismay, her mind faltered on finding a suitable explanation to follow.

When Frederick raised a questioning gaze to hers, she opened her mouth and let the words spill out, praying they would at least make sense. "The river comes in handy for things like that."

He held her gaze for another scrutinizing moment. "Your aunt's got some salve over here," he finally said. Turning, he sauntered around the table and opened the cabinet drawer adjacent to the china hutch.

While he retrieved the salve, Lillian swept her cloak off and hung it on a vacant peg next to the back door. Should she mention seeing him at the bridge? The hour was late, but she didn't know when she would get the chance to speak with him again alone. "The coffee smells good," she said as he handed the tin canister to her. "Did you make enough for two?"

His eyes crinkled. "Of course. It certainly beats drinking by myself."

Lillian withdrew cups and saucers from the hutch while Frederick retrieved the coffeepot from the fireplace. She waited until she and her uncle were seated across from each other at the kitchen table, the white light of the tallow and wax candle glittering between them, to seek an answer to her worrisome question. "Did you enjoy your walk this evening?"

He hesitated—only slightly, but enough for Lillian to notice—before taking the first sip. He waited until he set the cup back on its saucer before answering. "Saw me, did you?"

She paused with her own cup halfway to her mouth. "Yes. On the bridge. You looked like you were coming back from the Walkers' homestead." Casually, she took a small sip, resisting the urge to grimace. Uncle Frederick's coffee was much stronger than Aunt Emma's.

"I was." He folded his long arms on the table. "Jim Walker is a good friend of mine. He's also a nighthawk, like me. Sometimes when I can't sleep, I go out walking. If I see candlelight in Jim's window, I'll drop by for a visit." His wide mouth split into a grin. "His cousin makes a delicious johnnycake."

Why did her uncle's explanation sound too. . .simple? "I've met Ethan," she said. "Who is Jim?"

"Jim is Ethan's second cousin. He lives in the smaller of the two houses on the Walker homestead. Ethan shares the two-story house with his younger brother, Billy; twin sister, Emily; and her children, Jedidiah and Julie."

"Ethan's a twin?"

Frederick nodded. "So are his sister's children."

That bit of information about Ethan and his family brought a warm smile to Lillian's lips. When she noticed Frederick studying her with curiosity, she quickly concealed her maudlin expression. "Is it safe for you to go across the river?" she asked, getting back to her purpose.

He hooked his forefinger in his cup handle. "Everyone knows where I stand when it comes to the Cherokee and the removal. No one has given me any serious trouble over it yet."

"What about the pony clubs?"

His expression remained placid, but his eyes grew sharp and assessing. "Who told you about the pony clubs?"

"Honestly, Uncle Frederick, did you think I could live here for any length of time without finding out there's a band of outlaws going about terrorizing the Cherokee?" she asked, deftly avoiding answering his question.

"I had hoped you would."

"And why is that?"

"Because, I promised your father I would keep you out of harm's way and that I would absolutely not allow you to become involved in the conflict over the removal."

Given her father's concerns over her moving to Georgia amidst the removal conflict, she wasn't surprised he'd pressed Uncle Frederick to watch over her. "But, shouldn't my knowledge of the pony clubs only make me more aware of possible danger?"

"It didn't keep you in tonight," he quickly countered.

She lowered her gaze to the ghostly thread of steam rising from her cup. She should have known better than to think she could keep her meeting with Ethan, albeit unintentional, from her uncle. He was too astute, too perceptive.

"What are you not telling me, Lillian?"

She wanted to ask him the same thing, for she felt certain he was deliberately keeping something from her. But she suspected any inquiry pertaining to her suspicions would go unanswered.

Raising her lashes, she met his probing gaze. "I didn't know about the pony clubs before I left for my walk," she confessed. She went on to explain about Ethan seeing her walking along the riverbank, fearing she might be a member of the pony clubs, and coming to investigate. She left out the part about him scaring her half to death. "When I asked him what the pony clubs were, he told me." In the same breath she added, "He was a perfect gentleman, Uncle Frederick. He even needled me into promising not to venture out at night alone again."

To her surprise, Frederick's lips tipped in approval. "Ethan is a very nice young man."

Her tense shoulders relaxed. "Yes, he is. He's the one who cleansed my hands and lip. He was worried about the propriety of us being seen together at such a late hour. That's why I didn't mention running into him before."

Frederick gave a knowing nod. "That sounds like Ethan."

A meditative quietness fell between them while they each took a few cautious sips of the hot coffee. Her uncle apparently knew a lot about Ethan. Things she would like to know. Like, why were his eyes so blue? Where were his parents? Who taught him to speak so well, to walk so tall? But she feared if she focused too much on the enamoring Cherokee, she would reveal something she herself didn't even understand.

Setting down her cup, she turned her attention to something less specific; something that involved the entire Cherokee nation. "Uncle Frederick, this afternoon Aunt Emma said that most Cherokee families have already been driven from their homes by the new landowners. How have Ethan and his family managed to hold on to their homestead so long?"

"Because the man who holds the deed to the Walker homestead chooses not to take possession of the property until after the Cherokee are gone."

"Who is this man?"

He thought for only an instant. "I'm not really at liberty to say."

Lillian knew she could find out since deeds were public records. All she had to do was find out where the document was recorded. But what purpose would that serve, other than to allow her the opportunity to personally thank the man whose kindness allowed the rightful residents of the homestead to remain until their forced removal?

"So, what about the pony clubs?" Lillian asked, once again targeting her growing concern for her uncle's safety. "Doesn't your close association with the Cherokee put you in danger from the outlaws?"

Frederick leaned back in his chair, crossed his arms, and stared at the moon-sprinkled treetops outside the window. After a prolonged moment he looked back at Lillian, his face a mask of wavering shadows and planes in the candlelight. "Sometimes, Lillian, you have to do what you know in your heart is right, regardless of the consequences."

Renewed conviction shot through Lillian. Flattening her palms on the table, she leaned forward, stopping short of standing up. "That's exactly how I feel."

He halted her with an upheld hand. "Whoa, now, little lady. This is not your battle."

"But, surely there's something—"

"No!"

His sharp rebuttal sounded like a father scolding a defiant child. She pressed her lips together, swallowing her quick temper. After all, she reminded herself, he was her elder.

Deliberately, she eased back down in her seat and folded her hands in her lap. "Why?" she asked, forcing a calm tone.

Frederick refolded his arms on the table. "First of all, I promised your father—"

She opened her mouth to argue that her father wasn't there.

He stopped her with another raised hand. "Secondly," he continued his argument, "there is nothing you can do." A dark shadow of despair fell across his face. "There is nothing *any-one* can do. It's too late."

❧

Seated at her teaching desk, Lillian sealed her latest letter with one sharp rap from the side of her fist. For a month now, she had been writing letters to President Van Buren, members of Congress, Georgia's Governor Gilmer, and anyone else she could think of connected to the state and federal governments.

One month, and she hadn't received a single response to any of the written communications she had penned on behalf of the Cherokee.

She tucked the letter into her satchel along with her Bible and some papers she needed to grade that evening. She had dismissed the children an hour ago but had remained behind to write the letter. That morning, she had told Aunt Emma that she had some work to do at the school so her fretful aunt wouldn't send someone looking for her. Her relatives all thought she was wasting her time begging mercy from the government.

Maybe she was. But she didn't fancy hearing her kinsfolk telling her so. For that reason, she had taken to writing her letters in secret.

She slipped the satchel strap over her shoulder. Now to get to the post office and suffer another insolent look from the postmaster. Grabbing her shawl, she headed for the door.

Ominous clouds hovered low in the sky, imprisoning the dank moisture clinging to the air from a drenching rain the night before. As she set off on her trek to the post office, her mind drifted back over the past few weeks. Word had trickled in that Chief John Ross's final attempt at a protest against removal was failing, and federal troops would soon arrive to round up the Cherokee who hadn't removed themselves voluntarily from the land of their birth. Her heart ached just thinking about it.

She sidestepped a mud puddle. Uncle Frederick's nightly walks had also grown more frequent. She spent many restless nights herself, pacing her bedroom floor, and had heard his comings and goings at all hours of darkness. He had also taken to leaving for two and three days at a time, claiming he was visiting and carrying supplies to settlers who lived too far back in the mountains to make monthly trips into town.

And like an untreated infection, Lillian's suspicions had continued to grow. Something was going on. Something veiled in secrecy. Something, she strongly suspected, related to the Cherokee removal. But no one, not even Aunt Emma, would talk to Lillian about it. Every time she veered toward the topic of the intrusion, everyone else veered toward another, less harrowing subject.

So Lillian did the only thing she knew to do. She wrote letters. . .and prayed.

Lillian made quick work of delivering her letter, then strolled back past the school and toward Uncle Frederick and Aunt Emma's house along the river path. Because of the recent storm, the Chestatee swirled high on the riverbanks, its churning waters the muddy color of the Georgia red clay that formed the dirt streets of Adela.

As she neared the bridge and heard the children's laughter, an intense sense of grief swept over her. A grief heavier than yesterday's; perhaps not quite as heavy as tomorrow's.

Stopping in the midst of a soggy blanket of dogwood blossoms covering the ground, she watched the Cherokee children at play. Today, two additional youngsters had joined in the stickball game. Lillian figured they belonged to one of the adults working in the distant fields. The Indian neighbors shared the fields as well as the harvest. Lillian knew many white men who could learn from the benevolent spirit of the Cherokee.

The laughter of the children pranced through the clammy air, bringing a sad smile to Lillian's lips. They were happy now, but for how long? A few short weeks, maybe? The deadline for the treaty enforcement was the twenty-third of May, less than one month away.

Her gaze drifted farther down the stream, where she could see the big waterwheel turning, hear the pounding of the mill-stone, and glimpse the gristmill through the patchy openings in the trees. Ethan would be in there, grinding corn and wheat, providing sustenance for those who eagerly awaited the removal.

Lillian ground her teeth. They had a lot of gall, asking Ethan to process their grain so they could have fresh bread for their table. Why did he so willingly accommodate his oppressors? No doubt, he needed the few coins he received for his services.

Wrapping her arm around a shedding dogwood, she leaned against its rough trunk. She had seen Ethan twice since the night he had accompanied her home. The first time, he'd been walking from the gristmill toward his house. The last, he'd been playing with the children.

Both times, he'd ignored her.

Lillian was certain he had known she was there, standing at the mouth of the bridge; she had willed him to look her way so she could at least offer him a friendly wave. But he never would. And though she walked away on each occasion with a deep sense of disappointment, she understood. He had asked her to stay away, and he wasn't going to encourage her to do otherwise.

A shifting sense of awareness pulled her out of her dejected thoughts. Something in the atmosphere had changed. The laughter across the river had stopped.

She turned her attention back to the children to find their game had ceased, and one, two, three, four, five of them stood at the top of the opposite bank, looking down toward the swirling waters. Following their gaze, she found Jedidiah, Ethan's six-year-old nephew, balanced precariously on his stomach on a thin limb dangling out over the river. He was reaching for their game ball, which was lodged between two smaller branches extending downward and submerged in the churning waters.

"Jedidiah!"

Charging toward the child, she let the satchel slide off her shoulder and drop to the ground. She half-ran, half-slid down the riverbank, carrying a landslide of mud and rocks with her. She screamed the boy's name again when she reached bottom. Like the first time, he ignored her.

Jerking at the laces of her mud-slick boots, she glanced up the opposite bank. "Go get help!" she screamed to the oldest child, a boy.

The youngster looked at the little girl, barely more than a toddler, standing beside him. Apparently he was reluctant to leave his little sister.

Throwing off her first boot, she looked at Ethan's niece. "Julie, go to the mill and get Ethan. *Now!*"

The little girl took off running.

As Lillian slung off her second boot, the branch Jedidiah was clinging to snapped. A chorus of screams rose from the opposite bank.

"Sweet Jesus, no!" Lillian prayed, and somehow, miraculously, the child managed to hook his small fingers around the branch, which now clung to the tree by a thin sliver of bark—his lifeline. The murky waters pulled and tugged at the lower part of his body.

Lillian plunged into the river, fighting to keep her breath when the frigid waters consumed her to the waist. The water weighed down her dress and petticoats, twisting the material around her legs and ankles like a tangled rope. Trudging forward, she prayed the path between her and Jedidiah didn't get much deeper. She could swim—had learned in the plantation pond—but she doubted she could accomplish much against the swift current. At this depth, she could at least find footholds between the stones.

Halfway across, her foot slipped on a moss-covered rock.

She fell to her knees. The sharp edge of the rock ripped through her pantalets and stocking, and dug into her shin. She sank neck-deep in the chilly water.

She clawed frantically against the brutal current, trying to pull herself up. "Dear, God, please help me. Help Jedidiah." A handful of muddy water sloshed into her mouth. She gagged and sputtered to regain her breath. Bitter tears burned her eyes. She was losing the battle; both she and a child were about to lose their lives.

Dear God, she continued praying in silence, *if one of us must die today, please let it be me.* She knew her soul would be all right. But what about Jedidiah's? At six years old, she did not know if he could be accountable for his sins. And she didn't want to live the rest of her life wondering where he was if something were to happen to him. *Please, God, don't let that child die without first knowing You.*

A new surge of strength shot through her limbs. She found a foothold between two stones, pushed herself up, and continued her journey forward. She was almost within reach when the limb gave way completely. Diving forward, she caught the broken end of the branch with one hand. The bough began to slip. Splinters bit into her palm. "Hang on!" she screamed, as much for her benefit as Jedidiah's.

The child targeted her with a glazed look of terror. Drawing strength from his fear and desperation, she fought the relentless pull of the river and dug in her heels, managing to wrap her second hand around the limb.

She cut a quick glance toward the riverbank, a mere body-length away. So close, but it may as well have been a mile, because Lillian could do no more. The angry torrent of the river coupled with the struggling child on the other end of the branch was all the resistance she could handle.

"Lillian! Jedidiah!"

Lillian choked back a sob. *Thank God, Ethan is here.* He would save them both. Everything was going to be all right.

He ran down the bank, his movements as swift and smooth as a soaring eagle's.

"Get Jedidiah!" she said. "He's barely holding on."

Ethan eased into the water without a hitch in his movements. The motion drew Jedidiah's attention. When he saw Ethan, the child let go of the tree limb and reached for his uncle, but he was a split second too soon. Like a brisk wind catching a downy feather, the raging waters swept the youngster downstream.

"No!" Ethan and Lillian shouted in unison.

Lillian flung aside the tree branch and lunged forward, reaching for the boy. But the riverbed disappeared beneath her feet, and the ruthless waters of the muddy Chestatee swallowed her.

The tempestuous torrents tossed her to and fro, twisting her around in the black abyss of water. She reached but felt nothing solid. She kicked, only to find her legs bound by the heavy material of her dress and petticoats. She lost all sense of direction, of which way was up. . .or down. Then her left side and arm slammed into something hard and jagged. The air trapped in her lungs spewed out with force. All conscious thought began slipping away. Her weary body succumbed to pain and fatigue and went limp.

This was it. She was going home.

Dear faces drifted through her mind. First Ethan, then her father, then a six-year-old Cherokee boy.

She was going home. She hoped to see little Jedidiah there.

five

A strong arm wrapped around Lillian's waist, pulling her away from Oblivion's stingy grasp. Could it be the death angel had come to carry her home?

She felt herself shooting up, up, up, like a hurtling arrow, until. . .

She burst through the surface of the Chestatee. Hungry for air, she drew in a deep breath, but almost lost it when a sharp pain pierced her left side. She coughed and sputtered, discharging a large portion of the muddy water that she had swallowed.

Raising her uninjured arm, she swept a mass of hair away from her face and looked across the rippling clay-colored water. Someone was holding her back, fighting the pull of the current to keep her from being swept away—like Jedidiah.

Her eyes stretched wide in horror. Jedidiah! He was gone, and she was still here. It wasn't supposed to have happened this way. *"No!"* She struggled against her rescuer.

A second arm clamped around one side of her neck and beneath the opposite arm, trapping her against a solid chest and rendering her defenseless.

"No!" she repeated, pulling at the steely band across her neck and shoulder. "Jedidiah! We have to find Jedidiah!"

The arm tightened, forcing her head back against a hard shoulder. "Jedidiah is fine," Ethan said close to her ear. "Now stop fighting before you drown us both."

She ceased tugging at his arm but left her hands in place. What he said couldn't be true. She saw the boy being carried away by the water. "Promise?"

Great! Ethan thought. She picked a fine time to argue. His muscles were beginning to cramp from battling both her and the current.

"I promise," he ground out. "Now let me get you out, and you can see for yourself." To his relief, her body relaxed against his, and he swam the few treacherous feet to the bank.

When she had reached for Jed earlier, she had slipped into a deep crevice in the riverbed floor his people called the Raven Mocker's Hole, named for the mythical Cherokee spirits of death. The children had been warned repeatedly to stay away from it. Lillian had found out about it almost too late.

He crawled up on the shore, dragging her with him. She made a feeble attempt to help, but her limbs were so weak and her body so shaky, her efforts did little good.

Gathering her trembling body into his lap, he wrapped his aching arms around her. He was well aware they now had an audience. The neighbors who had been working the field and his sixteen-year-old brother had heard the commotion and now stood at the top of the embankment looking down at them. But, right now, he didn't care. He was going to sit there until he could feel Lillian's heart beating against his.

"How is she?" he heard his sister call from the top of the bank behind him.

"I. . .think," he said between heaving breaths, "she will be all right. . . . How's Jed?"

"He's safe. Just cold and frightened. I'm taking him inside to get warm and dry."

"Good. We'll be there in a minute."

"Can we help?" he heard one of his neighbors say.

"I think my brothers and I can see to her and Jedidiah's needs for now," his sister responded. "But we will certainly call upon you if you are needed. Thank you for your concern."

In a matter of seconds he sensed that he and Lillian were alone, thanks to his sister's insight. As their breathing steadied, a penetrating chill seeped into him, except where Lillian's body touched his. Even the delicate hand lying against his chest seemed to brand him with fire. He raised a palm to her tangled, muddy hair. A few stubborn hairpins still held together a remnant of her once-neat chignon. Resting his cheek on the top of her head, he closed his eyes. His mind spun with what had just happened, what could have happened, and the prayer he had prayed as he searched the dark, watery crevice for her.

Perhaps there was a merciful God after all.

A tremulous shudder passed through her. Instinctively, he tightened his arms around her, trying to absorb her shivering into his own body. When he heard her sharp gasp, he loosened his hold. "Are you all right?"

"Just cold," she answered, but her voice held the breathless strain of pain.

Angling his head so he could see her face, he gently tightened his arms again. She closed her eyes and bit her lower lip.

Fear gripped his stomach. "Where do you hurt? And don't try to tell me you don't."

"My left side. I think the current knocked me into a rock."

"I'm going to take you to my house. My sister will examine you and make sure you have no broken bones."

An even larger fear for Ethan was that Lillian may have internal injuries, like his grandfather had suffered when he fell while repairing their roof ten years ago. He had bled to death from the inside, and nothing anyone tried would stop it.

Gently, Ethan lifted her into the cradle of his arms, watching her face for signs of discomfort. Her saturated dress seemed to double the weight of her small frame, but determination lent new strength to his limbs, and he managed to carry her up the bank without drawing another grimace of pain from her.

"Is your sister a medicine woman?" Lillian asked as he plodded across the yard.

"Yes, but she doesn't practice conjuring and magic, as some of our medicine men and women do." Those arts did not align with his sister's Christian beliefs. "She can read illness and injury," Ethan went on to explain. "And she knows the healing powers of many plants."

"Oh," Lillian said, her tone telling Ethan she accepted his explanation without question, then she dropped her weary head to his shoulder.

He increased his pace, his soggy moccasins emitting little sound as his long strides ate up the yard. A hen that barely escaped one swinging foot flapped away squawking.

His brother had apparently been watching for them and opened the door. The sixteen year old was almost as tall and strong as Ethan, but the younger man's frame was leaner, not quite as sturdy as his older brother's.

Ethan didn't break his stride or stop to acknowledge anyone as he carried Lillian through the sitting room to the only bedroom on the main floor—his. The embers from the fire he had started that morning still glowed in the fireplace, spreading warmth throughout the spacious room. With his heel, he closed the door. After easing her down onto a straw-bottomed rocker, he reached for the top button of her dress, located at her throat.

Eyes rounding, she slapped away his hand. "Just what do you think you're doing?"

Ethan had expected her resistance. Undaunted, he propped his forearm on his raised knee. "I'm getting you out of those wet clothes so my sister can check your side."

"Oh, no you're not."

"Lillian," he said, using the same tone with her that he used with Jed and Julie when he had lost all patience. "If we don't get you out of that wet dress, you will take a chill."

"Then leave the room, and I'll take care of disrobing myself."

"Not until I know how badly you're hurt."

She curled her lips into a thin line. "As long as I am conscious, *I* will be the only one to remove my clothes."

Good thing she wasn't a man. If she were, he'd be tempted to render her unconscious and silence that rebellious tongue for a spell. "Lillian, I've seen a woman's body before."

He could see his statement took her aback, but she quickly recovered. "Not this woman's body."

Ethan raked a frustrated hand through his damp hair. This was ridiculous. What did she think he was going to do? Throw her down and devour her like a ravenous wolf? The only thing on his mind right now was finding out how serious her injuries were.

For a tense moment, their gazes locked in challenge. When she raised a dirty hand and grasped the front of her dress, where he had attempted to unbutton it, and lifted her mud-streaked chin an obstinate inch, Ethan threw up his hands in surrender. "Fine. If you promise to stay put, I'll go tend to Jed and send Emily to attend to you."

She opened her mouth to argue, Ethan suspected, that she was perfectly capable of attending to herself.

But he didn't give her the chance. "It's *me,* or her. Take your pick." And this time, he meant it. Fortunately, it didn't take her long to figure that out.

"Fine," she said. "But please don't ask Emily to leave Jedidiah until she is certain he's going to be all right."

Nodding, he started to stand.

"And, Ethan?"

He paused.

"I need to let Aunt Emma know where I am."

"I'll send my brother."

"Is it safe for him to go?"

Her profound concern for his brother drained away Ethan's aggravation. Mentally, he shook his head in awe. She had jumped into the raging Chestatee to save a Cherokee child's life without stopping to consider that, in the attempt, she could have lost her own. She did not know yet how serious her injuries were, yet she seemed more worried about him sending his brother to her aunt's house. How many others who lived across the river would do as she had done? Ethan could think of only two—three at the most.

"Yes, he will be safe," Ethan assured her, caressing her face. "He knows his way around."

She hesitated, her delicate brow creasing in contemplation, her right hand still curled unconsciously around the front of her dress. "All right," she finally said, as though he needed her permission to send his brother on the errand.

He took a few seconds to study her. Her hair was a tangled,

muddy mess, her face streaked with dirt, and her dress covered with river muck. Yet she maintained an air of dignity, and filled his eyes with a remarkable beauty he was just beginning to understand.

Rising, he ambled toward the door. He stopped in the sitting room and gave Billy instructions on what to tell Lillian's aunt—that Lillian had jumped in the river to save Jed, but both were all right, and he would bring her home after nightfall, when they were less likely to be seen by unfriendly foes of the Cherokee. Halfway up the stairs, he heard a dull thud coming from his bedroom. He raced back down the steps and flung open the door, and there lay Lillian in a crumpled heap on the floor.

❧

"Is she going to be all right?"

Seated on the edge of Ethan's bed, where Lillian now lay, Ethan's twin sister paused in wringing out a cloth over the washbasin. Aside from her raven-black hair, she was opposite Ethan in appearance, with a small frame, dark brown eyes, and fair skin.

"If you ask me that again," she said, "I will throw you out of the room."

Ethan glanced from Lillian's pale face to his sister's annoyed expression. She wouldn't throw him out of the room, even if she were big enough to try.

With a berating shake of her head, Emily proceeded to wash Lillian's face.

Probably one-half hour had passed since he'd found Lillian unconscious on his bedroom floor and carried her to his bed. Since then, he'd taken time to change into dry clothes and throw a few logs on the fire. Now he sat with her head cradled on his thigh, caressing her temple, watching closely every rise and fall of her chest.

He and his sister had managed to disrobe Lillian down to her chemise, but knowing how she would feel about her immodest state when she awakened, Ethan had covered her with a patchwork quilt.

Her breathing was steady and her heartbeat strong. No blood had drained from her mouth, like it had his grandfather's, and Emily had concluded that neither Lillian's left ribs nor arm were broken. Aside from a surface cut on her right leg, his sister could find nothing wrong. Yet Lillian had not stirred since he found her lifeless body on the floor, and with each passing moment, his fears increased. Had her lungs filled with water? Was there a wound inside her head that his sister couldn't see? Had he gotten her out of the water in time?

Finally, Emily finished cleaning Lillian's face and dropped the cloth into the washbasin. "Her color is good. She has feeling in her hands and feet. There's no bleeding inside, as far as I can tell. I think she just fainted."

The lack of concern in his sister's voice did nothing to ease his own apprehension. "Why would she do that?"

Emily shrugged one slim shoulder. "Perhaps she got up to get a blanket or to get closer to the fire, and the exhaustion from her fight with the river overwhelmed her."

Ethan looked down at Lillian's ashen face and swept the hair away from her brow. "I told her to stay put."

No response followed, and after a brief silence, he felt his sister's gaze boring into him. He glanced up and met eyes full of concern. His heart tripped. Had Emily found something wrong after all? "What is it?"

"You're in love with her," Emily said softly.

Ethan studied his sister's perceptive expression. His twin had always been able to read his thoughts, sometimes before he did. "Am I so obvious?"

"You look at her like your next heartbeat depends on her next breath, and touch her face like you're trying to memorize every line." Something akin to sympathy rose in Emily's eyes. "I know what love looks and feels like, Ethan. I also know how much it hurts when it's taken away."

He knew what she said was true. Two drunken gold miners had murdered her husband six years ago; Ethan thought, for a time, his sister would die of grief.

"Does she feel the same?" Emily asked.

"I don't know."

A brief but thoughtful silence passed. "What are you going to do?

The heavy hand of sorrow bore down upon his chest. What could he do? Between the pony clubs and the impending removal, his people were destined to suffer for years to come. He took a deep, painful breath, then answered his sister the only way he could. "I will do nothing. She doesn't belong with us."

Emily's dark eyes fill with compassion. "I understand."

Only another Cherokee would.

ঌ

"I'm going to make some poultice for her arm and side and some willow bark tea in case she needs something for pain when she wakes up," Emily said some minutes later.

Ethan nodded, grateful for the opportunity to be alone with Lillian and his own thoughts.

When the door closed behind his sister, he looked down at the woman whose head was still pillowed by his thigh. Almost losing her today had shed new light on his feelings for her. He was in love with her; he'd realized it the second he'd pulled her up onto the riverbank. But that new knowledge didn't make their situation any less impossible.

He brushed the backs of his fingers across her smooth cheek, noticing the sharp contrast between their complexions. His grandfather had been white. So had his father. In reality, only one-fourth of the blood running through his veins was Cherokee. But in his heart, he was Cherokee, and bound by the treacherous laws of a bogus treaty. The destiny of his people would keep him and Lillian apart. . .forever.

She stirred, turning her head so that her mouth brushed his fingers. Her balmy breath filled his palm. Warmth curled in his stomach. He caressed her lower lip with his thumb. If only the Treaty of New Echota did not exist. If only they had been born in a different time or of the same people.

When her eyes fluttered open, he pulled his hand away. Now he must put on a different face, for he could never let her know his feelings for her. To do so would only complicate both their lives.

She scanned the log wall and brick fireplace, then angled her head to look up at him. "What happened?"

He smiled. "You fainted. I picked you up and carried you to my bed."

Eyes widening, she glanced down and saw that only her chemise and a quilt covered her. Raising her uninjured arm, she pulled the cover up to her chin. Ethan suppressed a grin.

Peering up at him once more, she said, "How is Jedidiah?"

"He's fine."

"I remember seeing him pulled downstream. How did you manage to get him out?"

"His mother heard the children scream and arrived at the same time I did. She anticipated what could happen and ran downstream. Fortunately, she caught him."

Lillian's eyelids slid shut. "Thank God."

Noticing how easily the words slipped from her lips and the peaceful reverence on her face, Ethan was almost envious. Would there ever come a time when he could so freely thank God?

He felt an unsettling rise in his heartbeats. He'd felt it several times before, whenever he pondered God's existence, which he'd been doing a lot lately. He didn't like the tight feeling it brought to his throat, or the fear it planted in his stomach.

"What were you doing up?" he asked, hoping to steer his thoughts in another direction.

Her brow knit in thought. "I was cold. I wanted to get closer to the fireplace."

Guilt stabbed at him. "I should have given you a blanket before I left the room."

"I. . .ah. . .shouldn't have tried to get up."

He could see how hard it was for her to admit that perhaps she should have listened to him. A thick thread of sorrow needled him. What would it be like to spend his life with her? Certainly not boring or wearisome.

"Where are my clothes?" she wanted to know.

"Ruined. My sister will have something you can wear."

"When may I go home?"

He shook his head. "Not today, I'm afraid."

Instead of her usual rebellion, her eyes filled with question. "Why not?"

"Your left arm and side are badly bruised, and you have a cut on your right leg. You're also exhausted from your battle with the river and need to rest."

"But Aunt Emma will worry."

"We'll get word to her that you're going to stay the night."

"What about the pony clubs? If they learn I'm here, won't it put your family in danger?"

Once again, she thought of someone else ahead of herself. His chest swelled with an emotion he could not allow to surface on his face. He resisted the urge to caress her cheek. "We won't worry about that unless there is a need. The important thing is that we're all safe right now."

That night, after the house grew silent, Ethan tossed a blanket and pillow on the sitting room couch. He doubted he would get much sleep in his makeshift bed tonight. Visions of what had almost happened today, to both Lillian and Jed, still preyed upon his mind. And discovering the depth of his feelings for Lillian still had him a bit disconcerted.

Falling in love at this point in his life had not been in his plans, especially to a woman so far removed from his world. But it had happened—slipped up on him from behind. Now he would have to live with it for the rest of his lonely life.

He was about to blow out the candle on the small oak table next to the couch when he heard the restless shuffle and neighing of the horses in the corral. Pausing with his hand cupped around the flame, he listened. In a few seconds he heard the more distant sound of a horse and buggy crossing the bridge. Only one person would be crossing the river in a noisy carriage this late at night—Lillian's cousin, Thomas. And Ethan knew what he was coming for.

Ethan waited until he heard the attorney's footfalls on the

steps before opening the door. A lantern Thomas had attached to the front of his carriage illuminated the surrounding area in an eerie glow, making his shadowy figure appear like a ghost rising from the earth.

Thomas doffed his gray top hat as he stepped up to the door. "Ethan."

"Thomas."

The door to Ethan's right cracked open and Lillian peered out. Apparently, she had not yet fallen asleep and had heard Thomas drive up. When she saw the caller was her cousin, she finished opening the door and stepped up next to Ethan.

She had insisted on a bath that evening, and the result was shiny light gold hair cascading down her back and a face with a renewed healthy glow. She wore a red blouse, an indigo skirt, and buckskin moccasins she had borrowed from Emily.

"Thomas, what are you doing here?" she asked, her eyes stretched wide with surprise.

"I've come to take you home."

"She's injured," Ethan injected. "It isn't wise for her to travel so soon."

"It's even less wise that she stay here."

Ethan read the underlying meaning of Thomas's words. The longer Lillian stayed, the greater the risk of the wrong people finding out she was there. The greater the risks to his people. . .and to her. But should she leave, and something happen to her as a result, how could Ethan live with that?

She laid a hand on his forearm. "Thomas is right, Ethan," she said. "I should go with him."

Ethan looked down at her, her upturned face a soft, alluring glow in the flickering candlelight. "Lillian—"

"Ethan," she cut off his argument, "it's better this way."

"She's right," Thomas quickly followed. "I think you know that, Ethan."

Again, Ethan interpreted the unspoken message in the attorney's words. Should Lillian be seen with a man at such an hour, it would be better for her to be seen with her cousin than with a Cherokee. All the hopelessness and despair that had haunted Ethan for years surfaced with an explosive force. He couldn't even protect the woman he loved.

"I'll get you a blanket," he said, battling the need to hit something. "And the tea and poultice Emily made for you."

"I have a blanket in the buggy," Thomas said.

Without acknowledging Thomas's statement, Ethan turned and sauntered into the kitchen. When he returned, he handed a small medicine bag and a tin canister to Lillian. "My sister and I will never be able to repay you for what you did today."

"I simply reacted to a critical situation."

"You saved Jed's life."

She searched his face with lucid green eyes. "And you saved mine. That should make us even."

There was so much he wanted to say to her, and he sensed the same from her. But their opportunity would never come. When she walked out the door, she would walk out of his life. Forever.

He held her gaze for another fleeting moment, but no more for fear he'd reveal his innermost feelings. "Good night, Lillian."

She stepped over the threshold and took her place beside her cousin. "Tell Emily I'll leave her clothes on the bridge next Monday on my way to school."

"I'll look for them."

Thomas nodded. "Thanks for taking care of her."

"It was our pleasure."

As they started across the bridge, she looked back, her flaxen hair glinting like a beacon in the lantern light. Ethan raised his hand for one final wave, then quietly closed the door.

❧

As Thomas guided his horse across the bridge, Lillian looked back one last time. Ethan raised his hand for one final wave, then slowly closed the door.

The heaviness in her chest almost smothered her. The raw ache in her throat almost choked her. The bitter sting of tears rose in her eyes. She did not want to go home. She wanted to go back, for she was in love with Ethan Walker, and she would follow him to the ends of the earth if he would only ask.

Turning back around, she looked ahead, seeing nothing but imminent years of loneliness. She wasn't sure when it had happened, just that it had. And it was the kind of love she knew would stay with her for the rest of her life.

For a heartbeat, she thought of her former fiancé. What she had felt for him was nothing compared to what she felt for Ethan. In fact, she now wondered if she'd ever loved James at all.

"You have feelings for him," Thomas said, as though reading her mind.

"Yes, I do," she said, knowing her cousin was one of the few she could trust to keep her admission a secret.

At least five slow seconds slipped by. "I'm sorry you had to meet him at such an ill-fated time in history."

A silent tear trickled down her cheek. Pursing her salty lips, she drew in a deep breath, only vaguely aware of the pain in her side. "So am I." Her physical wounds would heal. Her heart never would.

six

Three weeks later, Lillian answered a knock at the front door and found a handsome man standing on the porch. Tall, broad-shouldered, with only a few strands of gray in the temple area of his thick, brown hair, Marcus Gunter wore officer's full dress attire, with the exception of his hat, which he held in one hand.

"Papa!" She threw herself into his arms.

Marcus Gunter spun his daughter around. "How's my princess?" he asked as he set her back on her feet.

"Better, now that you're here," she answered without thinking. When her father's brow dipped in concern, guilt pricked her conscience, and she wished she could take back her imprudent comment. With her hands, she framed his face, bristly from a day's growth of beard. "I can't believe you're here. Why didn't you write ahead and let me know you were coming for a visit?"

An even darker cloud shadowed his aristocratic features. "Actually, I'm here on duty."

Confusion pinched Lillian's forehead. "Duty?" The full meaning of his words sank in. The federal troops had arrived to enforce the treaty, and her father was to take part in the removal.

"No!" came her throaty protest. She stepped back, breaking contact. "Please tell me it isn't true."

"I'm afraid it is. I've been assigned to assist in the removal."

Her fragile world, held together by a thin thread of sanity over the past three weeks, began to unravel. "How could you?" Her voice rang with vehemence. She had never used such a tone with her father, and she could see a glimmer of shock and hurt in his expression. But his bewilderment did not temper her reaction. She was too shocked and hurt herself.

He stepped forward, extending a hand to her. "Lillian, I don't like this any more than you, but I've been given orders. I have no choice."

She inched back, just beyond his reach.

Halting his advance, he dropped his hand to his side, where the gilded hilt of his saber glinted in the late afternoon sun. "I didn't realize you would feel so strongly about this. I requested that I be assigned to the station near Adela, so I could spend a little time with you before the actual roundup begins. Perhaps I should have requested another location instead."

Lillian's fingernails dug into her palms. She knew, deep down, the grievous sense of betrayal she felt toward her father was misplaced. He wasn't to blame for the outrageous act about to take place. But the tangle of emotions squeezing the air from her lungs overpowered her rationality. All she could see was the two men she loved most, facing each other over opposite ends of a bayonet. "Perhaps you should have asked for a different assignment altogether," she quipped.

His disciplined shoulders drooped slightly in a gesture of regret and sorrowful resignation. "I did. My request was denied."

Like flood waters rushing through a breached dam, the anger fled Lillian's body, taking with it her last shred of fortitude. The past weeks of putting on a brave face while knowing Ethan would soon be gone, crumbled like a dead leaf crushed by a big, brutal hand. "Oh, Papa, it's so unfair." Tears clouded her vision, turning the gold-gilded epaulets on her father's blue uniform blurry.

He rushed forward, wrapping his strong arms around her.

She slipped her arms around his waist and accepted the support he offered. "So many Cherokee have already been burned out of their homes," she said. "They're living in the forests, surviving on what roots and berries they can find. Their children are starving. And those who have been fortunate enough to keep their homes live in constant fear of being visited by this ruthless band of outlaws called the pony clubs."

The words poured out of her mouth while she verbally

listed only a few of the immoral trespasses being committed against the Cherokee. "The Indians can't even testify against a white man in court. They're powerless to fight back against the intruders coming in and looting their homes.

"How, Papa? How can our government sit back and allow people to be treated in such an inhumane manner? It isn't fair," she repeated, her voice raspy with unleashed emotion. "It simply isn't fair." A heartrending sob raked across her body. Turning her face into her father's chest, she gave way to the well of tears burning her throat.

Raising a hand, her father cupped the back of her head. "I know, Sweetheart. I know." He held her until her weeping ebbed back into the deep ache that had grown inside her for the past few weeks, then he moved his hands to her upper arms and set her back until he could see her face. "Had I known I would find you in such an impassioned state, I would have never allowed you to come to Adela."

She released a withering sigh. "You try to protect me too much."

He brushed the back of a curled forefinger across one wet cheek and then the other. "Perhaps I do. But you are my daughter, my only child. If anything were to happen to you, I'd have no reason to go on."

Straightening her spine, Lillian drew in a deep, bracing breath. Her father had a grim and arduous task ahead—one she knew he didn't look forward to. She didn't want to be a distracting object of concern for him while he attended to his honor-bound duties. "Where will you set up the fort?"

"Two miles north of Adela."

Lillian lived with her aunt and uncle on the south side of town. She wasn't surprised her father had chosen the least populated side of Adela, away from the townspeople. . .and her. "When does the actual removal begin?"

"I haven't received those orders yet, but I'm sure it will be soon after the deadline."

Lillian knew the deadline for the Cherokee to comply with the treaty was May twenty-third, five days from today. She hooked her hand in the crook of her father's arm and led him inside. In a few days he, her own flesh and blood, would command his troops to go in and remove Ethan and his family from their home.

She must find a way to warn Ethan.

❧

The following afternoon, Lillian didn't linger at the church after she dismissed the children but headed straightaway for the path along the river. Right before she came into view of her uncle and aunt's house, she glanced around to make sure no one was watching, then slipped into the dense forest where the river veered southward. She knew if she followed the stream a short distance she would soon reach the back side of Ethan's homestead. She would then have to find a shallow place to cross the river, which shouldn't be hard to do. In spite of the heavy rain they'd received three weeks ago, the spring season had been unusually hot and dry. The area water levels were lower than normal.

When she caught the first glimpse of Ethan's home through the thickets and trees, she began looking for a crossing point and found one directly behind the house. On the opposite side of the river, the bank had long ago been dug away to form a gentle slope leading up to the backyard, apparently to make an easy path to the Walkers' water supply.

She trudged down the embankment, where she sat down on the rocky ground, took off her boots, and stuffed them into her book bag. Slipping the satchel strap over her shoulder, she stood and bunched her dress skirt in front of her, exposing her stockinged feet and legs below the knee. Then she eased into the river.

Cool water, clear as glass, swirled around her feet and rippled over the rocks like waltzing dancers. If the task before her were not so urgent and grim, she would seize a few minutes to stand in the middle of the river and enjoy the current tugging at her ankles. But she didn't have the time or the desire to engage in frolic with the removal so close at hand.

Looking down, watching each step, she picked her way

across the stream, smiling at a lazy fish swimming upstream.

As she started to step out of the water, she noticed a pair of moccasins planted directly in front of her. She could not straighten without either dropping her skirt in the water or exposing more of her legs, so, from a slightly stooped position, she allowed her gaze to drift upward. She scanned nicely filled out butternut-colored trousers, a green sash tied around a slim waist, an ivory-colored homespun shirt draped over broad shoulders, and finally met the volatile blue eyes of Ethan.

With his arms folded across his chest and his stormy expression, he looked just like he had the first time she met him, the day he forbade her to cross the bridge—sinfully handsome and dangerously alarming. Her heart tripped.

"What do you think you're doing?" he asked, his voice brimming with irritation.

"I need to talk to you," she answered, undaunted by his anger. She had expected it.

"No. You need to turn around and go home, where you belong."

"Not until you hear what I have to say."

He stood his ground like a mama bear guarding her cubs.

Lillian bristled. Why did the man have to be so hardheaded? She dropped the folds of her dress, allowing the bottom to fall into the water and pulled herself up to her full five-foot, two-inch height. "I mean it, Ethan. This is important."

"Important enough for you to put yourself in harm's way?" he snapped.

"Yes."

He glared down at her a contemplative moment, then reached out and captured her upper arm, helping her step out of the water. His firm but tender grasp spawned a giddy flutter beneath her ribs. He'd touched her so little, yet she'd missed it so much.

After she stepped onto dry land, Ethan scanned the forest across the river.

"No one followed me," she said.

"Let's hope not." He perused the trees once more, seemingly

searching every thicket, every shadow. "Let's go to the house, where we won't be seen."

He continued holding her arm while they trudged up the slope and walked across the backyard. Four corralled horses trying to escape the midday heat huddled in the shade of an oak tree, and two chickens pecked hungrily at the dry ground. What would become of the animals when Ethan and his family were gone? Would the new landowners inherit them? Or would the Cherokee be allowed to take their livestock with them?

They climbed three steps to a small stoop where Ethan opened the back door and stepped aside so Lillian could enter ahead of him.

She hesitated, glancing down. Red dirt clung to the bottom of her wet dress and stockings. Looking back up at Ethan, she said, "I'll mess up your floor if I go in."

A forlorn smile tipped one corner of his mouth. "I don't think that matters now." With the hand holding her arm, he urged her forward.

She stopped a couple of feet inside the door, leaning her satchel against the wall and waited for her eyes to adjust to the dim interior. When they did, she gaped around the room in shock. Everything was gone: the couch and table Ethan and his grandfather had made; his sister's hand-loomed rug; his grandmother's dream catcher that had hung over the mantle. Only a lone straw-bottom rocker sat next to the fireplace. Her questioning gaze darted to Ethan.

"We've sold almost everything we can't take along."

Tears warmed her eyes. Ducking her head, she strolled forward to the center of the room, the rustle of her dress as loud and unsettling as thunder in the stillness of the empty room. Although she fought her tremulous emotions, a teardrop escaped and trickled down her face. *It isn't fair!* she wanted to scream. *It isn't fair! It isn't right!*

Thinking of the man standing behind her, she wrapped her arms around her waist and remained quiet. The last thing he needed was to feel he must console her. *He* was the one who needed comforting. But, what could she say? *"I'm sorry this has happened, Ethan. Oh, by the way, my father will be here in a few days to escort you from your home."*

She pursed her lips, biting back the bitter laugh clawing at the back of her throat. In essence, that's exactly what she had come to tell him. What a cruel, cruel joke fate had played on them. Closing her eyes, she prayed for strength.

❧

Ethan stepped up behind her. He knew she was crying; he had seen the tears in her eyes before she turned away. His chest ached with an almost unbearable pressure. His arms hung heavy and empty at his sides. But he dared not touch her for fear of what would happen. They were both vulnerable right now, both in need of comfort from each other. If he got his arms around her, he wasn't sure he'd have the strength to let her go.

As though sensing his closeness—and his thoughts—she straightened her spine and wiped her face with her hands. "Where are Emily and the children?"

"Next door, helping Jim go through his things." Since Jim was a widower, Emily often helped him tackle the tasks a wife would normally do.

Lillian nodded, but didn't turn to face him.

He waited to see if she would initiate the conversation she felt a need to have with him. When she didn't, he softly asked, "What did you need to speak to me about?"

She drew in a deep breath, then released it slowly. "The troops are moving in."

Beneath all the fervent emotions tumbling through Ethan, a spark of irritation flickered. He knew the troops were moving in; he'd seen them. Surely she didn't risk coming out here to tell him that.

She turned, and the agony in her glittering eyes almost buckled his knees. A swell of need rose in his throat, threatening to choke him. He fought to keep his arms at his sides.

Hugging herself, like she was trying to hold in her own pain, she said, "But what you don't know is the man in command of the post in Adela"—at least three torturous seconds crawled by—"is my father."

Ethan's battered world tilted. "Your father?"

She nodded. "He's a colonel in the United States Army. When he was ordered to help with the removal, he asked to be reassigned elsewhere, but his request was denied. So he asked if he could set up his post close to Adela, so he could be near me. That request, his commanding officer honored."

"Then he will be the one who gives the order for his soldiers to break down our doors and drag us from our homes."

In a split instant, her eyes filled with tears again. "If there is resistance. Yes." She whispered the last word like that was all she could manage.

Shock gave way to blinding anger. A cold finger of betrayal circled Ethan's heart. "Is that what you came here to tell me, Lillian? That we should not resist but turn ourselves over voluntarily to your father?"

She flinched more than once at his sharp words. "No, Ethan, that's not what I'm saying at all."

"Then why did you come? Why did you tell me something I was better off not knowing?"

Her eyes pleaded for understanding. "I came because I wanted to warn you, so you can be prepared. And, because, when you found out my father's role in the removal, I did not want you to think. . ." She paused, her soft lips parted, like her next words were lodged in her throat.

"Think what, Lillian?"

She swallowed. "I didn't want you to think that I didn't care."

He wanted to believe her; wanted to with every fiber of his being. But could he? How could he know she wasn't there on behalf of her father, trying to find out if Ethan and his family planned to resist, or if they were armed?

He pivoted and stalked to a back window. He stared out at the knee-high corn in the field, the cabbages and onions, the beans that were beginning to sprout. . . Did she know who would harvest those crops? Who would one day own this land?

He drew in a deep, painful breath. Perhaps she did. Perhaps

the inheritor of the homestead had promised her a fair share in exchange for her help in seeing that Ethan and his family left everything intact and prospering.

Perhaps. . . . His shoulders slumped in dejection. Perhaps, if he could make himself believe that, he could someday forget her.

His anger vanished like a vapor in the wind. Wearily, he scrubbed a hand down his face. Lillian wasn't there on a mission of deceit. All he had to do was look at her to know that. She wore her feelings on her face, held nothing back. She wasn't capable of treachery any more than he was capable of forgetting her.

"They will circle the house and approach from all sides to prevent anyone from escaping," she said from close behind him.

He'd been so entranced by his own disconcerting thoughts, he hadn't even sensed her approach.

"They will knock on the front door," she continued to explain the imminent scene ahead of him. "If no one opens it, they will force their way in. They will escort you to a depot that is being built at the local fort. You will stay until the roundup in this area is complete. Then you will be transferred to one of two general locations where you will be turned over to the Superintendent of Cherokee Immigration to await deportation."

For a few suspended seconds, an agonizing silence hung between them. Then her skirts rustled, and Ethan felt the slight disturbance of the stale air as she walked away. Out of the corner of his eye, he saw her pick up her satchel and reach for the door.

He turned his head and looked at her. "Lillian."

With her hand on the doorknob, she paused and met his gaze.

"Why are you telling me this?"

"Because I do care, Ethan. About your people. . .and about you."

The heartrending tenderness in her face told him all he

needed to know. The words "I love you" had never passed between them, but they were there, just below the surface, begging for release.

"And your father?" he inquired. "Does he know how you feel. . .about the removal?" The last he added to clarify his question. He felt certain her father didn't know Lillian's feelings went beyond ethical compassion for the Cherokee.

"Yes. He knows how I feel about the removal, and his part in it." Releasing the doorknob, she stepped up to him. "Ethan, he doesn't approve of the removal himself, but he's been given a direct order. He has no choice but to carry it out."

"Everyone has a choice, Lillian."

She searched his face with a benevolence he could almost physically feel. "Did you, Ethan?" she asked softly. "When those twenty men signed that treaty, and the United States ratified it, did they give you a choice?"

Yes. He had been given a choice. It was forced upon him, and had been a hard one to make. But it was *his*. His and his family's.

Lillian didn't know that, though. And he wasn't sure he should tell her. She trusted people he didn't, and could let something slip unintentionally.

"Were a soldier to disobey a direct order," she added, "he would bring dishonor to his uniform, and break the oath he made to serve his country. It would be like you pledging allegiance to the state of Georgia and denying your Cherokee heritage."

Her compassion and insight amazed him. Her strength astounded him. She was caught in the middle, between two men she loved. Yet, she had taken a clear stand and spoken out against what she felt was unjust. He offered her a sad smile. "You're a remarkable woman, Lillian Gunter. Fate has dealt us both a losing hand."

She swallowed—hard. For a minute, Ethan thought she was going to cry again. But she didn't. Her eyes grew misty, but no tears fell. It was as though she was resigning herself to what must be. "Yes. It seems it has."

Turning to face her, he presented her his arm. "Come, *aquatseli Liliyani,* I'll walk you home."

ەھ

The following morning, the pink twilight of dawn found Lillian tugging on her boots. She had awakened hours ago with an idea and couldn't wait to share it with Ethan. After quickly pinning up her hair, she grabbed her satchel, which was weighed down with her Bible and two textbooks, and quietly made her way through the house. If she left now, she'd have plenty of time to make the trek to the Walker homestead and get to the church before the children arrived for their lessons.

She slipped out the back door, her steps a little lighter than yesterday's. Why hadn't she thought of this before? After all, with an estimated fifteen thousand Cherokee emigrating to the Arkansas Territory, there would be a need for more schools—and more teachers.

Birdsong flitted through the air. Squirrels scampered through the trees. Wildflowers bowed their dewy heads like saints in humble reverence. It had been a long time since she had noticed the beauty of a clear spring morning. Too long.

She stepped off the path where the river veered southward. She hoped Ethan would be pleased with her news. It wouldn't make the forced removal any less treacherous, but perhaps it would give him something to look forward to, a small glimmer in the obliterating darkness now surrounding him.

She knew he cared for her. Even though he hadn't said as much, she could see it in his eyes when he looked at her, feel it in his touch each time he reached for her. She'd never experienced anything like it before—this bonding of spirits that couldn't be explained. Her mother used to talk about it; that special love so many looked for but so few found. With a faraway look in her eyes, she would say: "When you find it, my dear daughter, don't let it pass you by, for you never know if there will be another tomorrow."

Earlier that morning, Lillian had decided to take her mother's advice.

A sound that didn't fit the songs of nature penetrated her

entrancing thoughts. Stopping, she listened. Almost immediately she noticed the birds had stopped singing and the squirrels had all run for cover. Uneasiness prickled the back of her neck. Something wasn't right.

A garbled sound, like hysteria trapped in someone's throat, broke through the silence. A man's voice, too low and far away for clarity, followed. Then there was a rustling sound.

Trepidation riding on her back, Lillian followed the noises, clawing through low tree branches and lumbering over dense undergrowth. The disturbance led her away from the river, over a small knoll, and down to a heavy laurel thicket.

"Hold her arms," came the man's voice again. "I need to pin down her legs. She's buckin' like a mule with a burr under her saddle."

"It'll jes' make the ride more fun," said another man.

A wicked-sounding chuckle followed.

With her heart lodged in her throat and a fist of fear pounding on her chest, Lillian peered around the thicket, and what she saw sickened her.

Two men held down a young girl, one of Ethan's neighbors. One man held her arms over her head; the other had trapped her legs beneath his knees and was poised over her with a knife, ready to slit the front of her dress. She couldn't have been more than fifteen. With her mouth gagged by a bandana and tears streaming down her temples, she struggled frantically against her captors.

A third man stood back, leaning against a tree with his arms and ankles crossed, watching casually like he had nothing better to do. A dark, wide-brimmed felt hat sat low on his brow, and a red bandana covered his face below his shaded eyes.

The scene lit a fire of rage inside Lillian. Grasping the strap of her heavy satchel with both hands, she charged toward the men holding the girl. "Noooooo!" She drew back the bag and swung with a force born of wrath, catching the man who held the knife on the side of his head. He dropped his weapon and rolled away holding his ear.

Like the arm of a mighty pendulum, she brought the bag

back up, hooking the other man, who was now gaping like a fish, underneath his chin. He tumbled backward.

"Run!" she told the young girl.

In a dazed stupor, the girl blinked up at Lillian.

"I said 'Run!' Get out of here! Now!"

Apparently snapping out of her shock, the girl scrambled up and fled.

Lillian swung at the third man, who had pushed away from the tree and now rushed toward them. He raised an arm, deflecting the blow.

Dropping her bag, Lillian turned to flee. Like a striking snake, he reached out and grabbed her wrist, jerking her back and twisting her arm behind her back. She caught a glimpse of the young girl disappearing over the knoll, and a brief prayer of thanksgiving flitted through Lillian's mind.

In spite of the burning pain shooting through her arm, she struggled with her captor. "Help! Help! Somebody! Please!"

"Shut up," the masked man sneered close to her ear. "Trust me. You don't want me to have to do it."

Stunned by the familiar voice, Lillian stopped struggling. It couldn't be!

"Come on," he told the other two addled men clambering up off the ground. "Let's get out of here before that Indian comes after her."

Shock gave way to reality, and a sick feeling boiled in the pit of her stomach. She had trusted this man with some of her innermost feelings, and he had betrayed her. He'd even betrayed his own parents. . .and the Cherokee.

The name thrust from her chest, pushed past the bile in her throat, and spewed from her lips in disgust.

"Thomas."

seven

"Someone is coming," Ethan and his brother said in unison.

Ethan shot Billy a quick glance across the quilt spread over the floor, which now served as their kitchen table.

A plate of hot biscuits in hand, Emily stopped midway between the kitchen fireplace and the blanket. Her dark eyes widened in alarm. "Soldiers?"

"No." Ethan laid his fork on his plate. "It's too soon. But, whoever it is, they're approaching from the back." He pushed up from the floor and strode from the room. Billy followed close behind.

When Ethan stepped out the back door, he found his neighbor's oldest daughter running from the river like a wild bear was chasing her, a bandanna hanging around her neck. Dread tightened his chest. In spite of repeated warning from her parents about the pony clubs, the young woman sometimes slipped off to bathe in the river.

Ethan jumped the steps and ran across the yard, meeting her halfway. He grabbed her shoulders, stopping her from plowing into him. Tears streamed down her dirty face. Leaves and pine needles clung to her tangled hair. One sleeve of her dress was torn.

"Tralyta, what happened?"

A retching sob tore from her throat.

Gently but firmly, Ethan shook her. "Tell me, Tralyta, did someone hurt you?"

She slung her head from side to side. "No," she wailed in her native tongue. "The teacher. The teacher. They have the teacher."

Fear gripped Ethan's stomach. Of their own volition, his fingers tightened on Tralyta's shoulders. "Who has the teacher?"

"The men! The men!"

Emily appeared at Tralyta's side and draped a blanket over the young girl's shoulders. "Come. Let's get you inside."

As his sister led Tralyta away, Ethan turned to Billy. "Saddle Black Thunder," Ethan said, then stormed toward the house while his brother ran for the barn.

Inside his bedroom, Ethan pushed aside a chest of drawers—one piece of furniture he had refused to sell—and opened a hidden door in the floor. From the obscure compartment, he withdrew a rifle, a bow, arrows, and his hunting knife, none of which he was supposed to have according to federal law. The Cherokee had been disarmed after the New Echota treaty was ratified to prevent an uprising in protest of the impending removal. But Ethan had held back a few weapons. How else was he supposed to protect his family from the vigilantes that had rained terror on his people for years now?

He placed the weapons on his mattress, which now lay on a bare floor, and was sliding the chest of drawers back over the hidden door when Emily stepped into the bedroom doorway. She paused, her hand on the frame. "You're going after her," she said. It was a statement, not a question.

"Yes." He checked his gun barrel.

"They could kill you."

Ethan snapped the rifle closed. He knew what she said was a very real possibility. He also knew if anything happened to Lillian, living the remainder of his life knowing she was gone would be a fate worse than death. "How is Tralyta?" he asked, sheathing his knife in the leather casing attached to his belt.

Emily stepped further into the room. "Physically, she's fine. They didn't hurt her."

"Good. Was she able to tell you what happened?"

"There were three of them. Two were about to rape her when Lillian, it seemed, appeared out of nowhere and beat them off with her satchel. She ordered Tralyta to run, but the third man grabbed Lillian before she could get away."

Ethan wasn't surprised. Lillian was quick to put herself in harm's way for the sake of others, a fact that both enhanced his respect for her—and scared him half to death. "Where?" he wanted to know.

"Across the river and over the knoll, about halfway between here and Reverend Price's house."

Ethan knew the villains would be gone with Lillian when he got there, but at least he would have a starting place. He slipped the bow and arrow-filled quiver over his shoulder. "As soon as you get Tralyta home, you and the rest of our family must leave. You should be able to reach the Eagle's Nest by sundown. If Lillian and I are not there by sunrise tomorrow, go on without us. We'll either catch up or meet you in the valley."

"But—"

"When Lillian doesn't show up at school this morning, suspicions will arise," he continued, intercepting his sister's argument. "If Thomas is among those who abducted her, he will kill her to keep her from identifying him, then he'll point the finger of blame at me. If you stay here, the Georgia authorities will hold you hostage until I turn myself in."

Ethan had not forgotten Lillian's father was in Adela with a regiment of troops under his command. Ethan suspected that when the colonel found out his daughter was missing, he wouldn't stop searching for her until he found her—or drew his last breath.

Ethan understood. Neither would he.

With a forlorn expression of acceptance, Emily nodded.

Ethan cupped her cheek with his hand, offering her a pensive smile. "We've known for some time this day was coming."

"Yes. But I didn't know it would happen this way. I don't want to lose you."

"I don't want to lose anyone, either."

"Especially Lillian."

A silent message of understanding passed between them. Emily had once known the kind of love Ethan had recently discovered. She knew the turmoil Ethan was feeling, the sacrifice he was willing to make. If he lost his life trying to save Lillian's, so be it. The battle would not be in vain.

"I know you're in a hurry to be on your way," Emily said. "Jed and Julie are preparing some biscuits and a canteen of water for you. . .and Lillian. I'll go get them and bring them outside to you." She turned away, but not before he caught a glimpse of the tears welling up in her eyes.

Without pause, Ethan strode outside where Billy was tying a blanket to the back of Black Thunder's saddle. Ethan sheathed his rifle, then mounted the midnight gelding.

Emily came rushing out the back door clutching a small cloth bag and a canteen. He took the water vessel and wrapped the strap around the saddle's pommel while Emily stuffed the sack of biscuits into his saddlebag.

Forcing a smile, he winked at Jed and Julie who were standing on the stoop. Then he met and held his twin's gaze for a fleeting moment.

"I will pray," she said. "For both of you."

He nodded, and started to kick his horse into action, but hesitated when he caught sight of Billy coming out of the barn astride his sorrel mare. "What do you think you're doing?" he asked the younger man as he reined in his horse beside Black Thunder.

Billy met Ethan's glower with steadfast determination. "I'm going with you."

"But your sister—"

"Will have Jim and the children to travel with her."

Ethan clenched his teeth. He didn't have time to waste on arguing. Even if he did forbid Billy to come, the youth would probably follow anyway. "All right, then," he ground out. "Let's go." He heeled Black Thunder into a swift gallop. Billy trailed by a neck-length.

They found signs of a struggle exactly where Tralyta said the skirmish had taken place. They also found Lillian's satchel with its contents dumped on the ground. They stopped to retrieve the bag and scattered books and to pick up the trail of the villains. Billy scooped up the two schoolbooks; Ethan recovered the satchel and the Bible.

When he picked up the testament, he noticed the worn feel

of the leather binding, the curled corner of the pages that had obviously been turned numerous times. His throat clogged with emotion as he caressed the cover with his thumb. Lillian loved that book, had worried herself silly about it until Billy retrieved it from the riverbank the day she and Jed were pulled from the Chestatee.

"Lillian," Billy said. "She is a Christian?"

"Yes."

"Then, if anything happens to her, she'll be in heaven."

Ethan blinked, his brother's comment jerking him out of his trance. What was he doing? He needed to be on the outlaws' trail, not wasting precious seconds looking into a memory. "We'd better get going."

&

Lillian turned her head to dodge a limb, which was all she could do with her wrists tied to the pommel. Thomas sat on the horse behind her, his arms trapping her upper body like the jaws of a guillotine. He drove his mount fast and hard uphill, his two allies following close behind. They had been traveling, at the most, twenty minutes, and already the animals were lathered.

The tree branch raked through Lillian's hair, dislodging a hairpin. Surely this was a dream, a horrible nightmare from which she would soon awaken. But the ropes biting into her wrists, the lurching sway of the horse beneath her, and the repulsive feel of her cousin's body against her back told her differently.

She wasn't dreaming. Thomas really was a member of the pony clubs, and from the way his two accomplices called him "Boss" and took orders from him, he was obviously a very prominent member. And since she could identify him, he would never allow her to return to Adela alive. Grief and sorrow burned her throat. She would never see her father. . .or Ethan again.

How could she have been so blind? She had been completely taken in by Thomas's pleasant façade. She dodged another limb. Thomas released a harsh oath when the bough slapped him in the face. At least she could find a small degree of satisfaction in his discomfort.

There were a dozen questions she wanted to ask him, the first being: "Why?" But the ride was too rough for her to do anything but dodge branches and concentrate on staying upright in the saddle. They rode approximately five more minutes, then stopped in a small, level clearing where the mountain peaked.

"Let's hurry up and get this done," Thomas said, swinging off his horse. "As soon as they discover she's missing, they will come to me to help find her. I need to be back in town by then."

"Ye mean ye know her, Boss?" asked Bud, the stockier of the other two men. He wore a ragged beard and his dirty clothes reeked of old perspiration.

Thomas yanked at the ropes binding her wrists. "She's my cousin."

His voice was harsh and thick with vindictiveness she had once thought him incapable of. Where was his infectious smile? His buoyant good humor?

"You mean you're going to kill your own cousin?" the tall, lean assailant called William asked. He spoke with an educated southern drawl, and his clothes were well tailored and more neatly laundered than Bud's.

Lillian suppressed a bitter laugh. An attorney, a dandy, and a filthy derelict. Obviously, evil came in all sorts of disguises.

"What other choice do I have?" Thomas sneered. "She can identify us, and her father is the colonel in charge of the removal troops in this area. What do you think he will do if he finds out we abducted his daughter?"

Offering no further argument, William and Bud swung down off their mounts. They had all pulled down their bandanas by now, exposing their repugnant faces.

Thomas freed Lillian's wrists from the pommel, but not from each other. Ignoring the hands that reached up to help her, Lillian grasped the pommel as best she could and slid from the horse unaided. Still, Thomas grasped her waist and eased her the last few inches to the ground. Why did he bother? He was going to kill her anyway.

Turning to face him, she looked deep into his eyes, searching for the man she thought she knew. His gaze was cold, his features menacing. Obviously, this was the true Thomas. He had been a wolf in sheep's clothing all along. "Why, Thomas? Why are you part of such a corrupt lot?"

"I don't have time to explain." He grasped her upper arm and propelled her toward the ledge.

So that's how he intended to dispose of her, by throwing her over the cliff. She planted her feet firmly on the ground, resisting. "I deserve to know why I'm going to die."

He stopped abruptly, fingers digging into her arm, and whipped her around to face him. "Because I don't like Indians. They're worthless. They don't even make good slaves."

"You mean, you would burn a man out of his home and kill and rape his children because of his race?"

"That. And to gain possession of what is rightfully mine."

"What are you talking about?"

"The land, Lillian. The property your Indian boyfriend lives on belongs to my father. Three gold lots. One hundred and sixty acres sitting on the richest gold vein in the region, and he won't let me touch it until the Cherokee are gone."

Lillian's head spun with confusion. "You mean, Uncle Frederick took part in the land lottery?" She couldn't believe the minister would participate in such a treacherous act.

A sardonic smile pulled at Thomas's mouth. "The righteous Reverend Price? Take part in a lottery? Heavens, no. He protested it. When it took place anyway, he searched out the owners of the three lots across the river and bought them. Said he wanted to provide a City of Refuge for the Walker family and the other Indians in this area who were forced out of their homes before the removal. He even petitioned the government to allow the redskins to stay after the removal. He may have succeeded, too, had I not intervened."

Then he shook his head. "A City of Refuge, Lillian. Imagine that. This"—he made a wide sweep with his free hand—

"is not Jerusalem. It's not Indian Territory anymore either. It's Georgia. And when your father finishes moving those lowly beasts off the property across the river, my father will no longer have a reason to keep it from me."

"So you pretended to work for the Cherokee when you were actually working against them."

A leering grin widened his mouth. "You catch on quickly; much more so than Mother and Father." His cold eyes yielded to a look of deep regret. "I'm so close, Lillian. Just a few more days. I've worked years for this, and I won't let anything—or anyone—get in my way now. Not even you." He raised a hand to caress her cheek.

She recoiled.

He dropped his hand. When she ventured to look at him again, his nostrils were flared. His hate was potent. So potent, it brushed Lillian's body with a heinous chill. She had never been in the presence of such evil. She could almost see the demons rising from the ground, dancing in celebration of their latest sacrifice—her.

In that instant, she imagined she knew how Ethan must feel to be persecuted at the hands of friends who had betrayed him. Tears of heartache and desolation clouded her vision.

"I'm sorry it has to be his way, Lillian," Thomas said. "You should have listened to me when I told you to stay away from the Indians."

"God have mercy on your soul, Thomas," Lillian rasped.

He spun her back around and shoved her toward the ledge. His grasp, both cruel and merciful, held her back from falling.

She looked down and her knees seemed to vanish. Her stomach lurched and her heart leapt to her throat. The drop-off was straight down and seemed endless. Jagged rocks protruded from the cliff wall. No one could survive such a fall. A body lying at the bottom of the chasm could be lost forever among the heavy underbrush.

The wind whipped her hair and dress. Somewhere above, a raven released a harrowing caw that echoed through the canyon—a death call.

Drawing in a deep, bracing breath, she raised her head and glared at Thomas. "You don't intend for anyone to find me, do you?"

He feigned a regretful expression, but his eyes remained cold and vicious. "I'm afraid not. That way, I can convince the authorities that Ethan took you. After all, the man is rather taken by you. Even my father will attest to that."

Fear crystallized instantly into red-hot anger. "You mean, you intend to frame Ethan for this?"

"That's exactly what I intend to do. Maybe Father will open his eyes and see he's wasted all his time and money on the redskins for nothing."

A blinding surge of strength took possession of Lillian. She whipped around, bringing up her bound hands and catching Thomas on the jaw. Releasing her arm, he teetered sideways. Lillian ran for the opposite side of the clearing.

William and Bud, taken aback by her sudden action, delayed reacting by a split second. She managed to sidestep Bud, whose weight restricted his agility. But William, standing further back, snaked out one long arm and captured her, jerking her back and pinning her against his chest.

She struggled until William ruthlessly tightened his hold, squeezing her ribs and cutting off her breath. Gray spots floated before her eyes. Amidst those swimming blotches, she saw Thomas storming toward her, his face skewed with malevolence.

"You witch!" he growled. He raised his arm, clearly intending to backhand her.

Before she could react, a sharp crack ripped through the air. Something kicked up the dirt less than two inches in front of Thomas's feet. Everyone froze, their gazes snapping toward the edge of the clearing.

"Ethan," Lillian muttered, her legs buckling from relief, but her captor's taut arms kept her from crumpling to the ground.

Ethan stood, bold and tall, a rifle propped against his shoulder, Thomas his target. "Lay one hand on her, Price, and I'll take your head off." His voice was low—and deadly calm.

Thomas dropped the hand poised to strike and shuffled to the side, positioning Lillian and William between him and Ethan. He peered around them enough to maintain eye contact with Ethan. "From where I stand, I see three of us and one of you. Who's going to help you?"

Like breaking glass, the click of a gun hammer crackled through the air. "I am." Billy's voice came from behind Lillian, where he had a clear shot of both Thomas and William.

Thomas glowered at Bud. "Where's your rifle?"

The hefty man's gaze shifted to the horses, which stood along the edge of the plateau, close to Ethan.

Thomas spat an offensive name Bud's way. "How could you have been so stupid?"

Slowly, Bud started easing backward, toward the trees.

"Don't try it, Bud," Ethan said without taking his eyes off Thomas.

Bud stopped.

Ethan shifted his gaze to Lillian. "Are you all right?"

She nodded.

He then looked at William. "Let her go. . .easily."

Her captor glanced at Thomas, as though seeking permission.

"My brother's gun is pointed directly at your back," Ethan said. "You don't need anyone's permission but mine."

The man's arms fell away from Lillian's upper body. Amazingly, her shaking legs supported her. She ran to Ethan, who swept her behind him with one arm.

Ethan motioned to Bud. "Get over there with your friends."

Raising his hands, presenting his palms to Ethan, Bud scurried over to his partners.

"Now, all of you, line up where I can see you," Ethan added, "and keep your hands in the air."

Gun to shoulder, his aim unwavering, Billy sidestepped until he stood next to Ethan. The scene reminded Lillian of a firing squad, but surely Ethan and Billy didn't intend to shoot the villains.

"Lillian," Ethan said. "I want you to walk downhill, about

two hundred feet. You'll find our horses there."

An uneasy feeling of foreboding fingered her spine. "Why? What are you going to do?"

"Just go, Lillian."

A quiver of alarm rocked her. He was going to shoot them, after all.

"You can't kill us," Thomas said. "We're unarmed."

"Last I heard, kidnapping and attempted rape were crimes worthy of death." Slowly, deliberately, Ethan pulled back the hammer on his gun.

Lillian laid a hand on his arm. "Ethan, no. Don't do it."

"They deserve exactly what they intended to do to you, Lillian. Now, please go."

"Let the law deal with them."

"Don't you understand, Lillian? They are the so-called law in this area. No one will take an Indian's word against a white man's. Their crimes will go unpunished, just like all those they've committed in the past."

"Then let God deliver judgment."

A heavy silence dropped over the clearing. Not a leaf rustled, not an animal stirred.

"They will have to stand before God someday," Lillian added softly. "Just like you and I will."

They will have to stand before God someday. Just like you and I will. The words clawed at Ethan's mind, hammered at his conscience. He had never taken another man's life. Yet, the years of strife and torture of his people—of his very own mother—at the hands of reprobates like Thomas, Bud, and William haunted Ethan, pressed upon him until his finger was a breath away from pulling the trigger.

Here was his chance to avenge a few of the persecutions inflicted on the Cherokee. And how better to do it than through a man he once trusted, a man he had once called "friend"—a man who had betrayed him? He stared down the barrel of the gun, heart pounding in his ears, the balance of indecision bending toward vengeance.

"It's up to God, Ethan. Not you or me."

Lillian's pleading voice tunneled through his vindictive thoughts.

"You have a choice," she added. "Please make the right one."

The right one? Did she realize what the "right" choice meant for her? "Lillian, if I don't kill them, you can't return to Adela. Your life will be in danger as long as Thomas lives."

"I know," she responded.

"You will have to go with me and my family until we can figure out a way to get you safely home to Virginia."

She hesitated only slightly. "Yes."

"By the laws of your people," he said, "I will be considered a fugitive."

"I know. I also know that whatever you decide to do, you must decide for yourself, not for me. It's a decision you will have to live with. Either way, I'm not going back to Adela. I'm going with you."

Shock squeezed his ribs. Did she just say she was going with him, no matter what he did? Both excitement and dread tangled together inside him. He wanted her with him; wanted it more than anything. But she didn't realize what lay ahead for him and his family. Once she did, how would she feel about her decision to go with him?

He had no time to reason with her right now. People would be scouting the woods soon, looking for her. He had to do whatever he was going to do and be on his way.

"Take off your clothes," he told the three outlaws.

William swallowed, his protruding Adam's apple bobbing above his stiff collar and string tie. Bud released a dumbfounded "Huh?" And Thomas said, "You can't be serious."

"I've never been more serious about anything in my life. Now take them off."

The two men looked to Thomas. Thomas, in turn, did not move, just leveled Ethan with a look of utter disdain.

Ethan lowered the gun barrel and fired. The bullet kicked up the dirt between Thomas's feet.

Thomas did a quick two-step trot, then began pulling off his boots. Bud and William followed suit.

"Lillian, you may want to turn around," Ethan said.

Out of the corner of his eye, Ethan thought he saw her lips twitch, like she was trying to suppress a grin. Then she turned around.

"Now, throw your clothes over the cliff," Ethan ordered after the men had stripped naked.

"All of 'em?" William asked.

"Better them than you, don't you think?"

"How do you expect us to get back to town like this?" Thomas wanted to know.

"That, Mr. Price, is your problem. Billy, get the horses."

Bud, cowered over and covering himself with his hands, looked like someone was snatching a plate of food out from under his nose. "You ain't takin' the horses, too, er ye?"

"Yes," Ethan answered. "We certainly are." He narrowed his eyes at Thomas, sending him a silent message. "After all, at least one of them came from my corral."

Satisfied that the outlaws would not soon follow, Ethan captured Lillian's upper arm and guided her down the mountain toward their mounts.

To his surprise, she glanced back, then quickly faced forward. Pursing her lips, she fought mirth, but an effervescent giggle bubbled up from her chest and escaped anyway.

Ethan couldn't help smiling. He wished the road before him didn't look so grim, that there was a promising place in his life for her. But nothing about his future looked promising.

"Little brother," he said, determined to hang on to the fleeting spirit of gaiety as long as possible, "I fear we've just captured ourselves a hellion."

eight

Kneeling beside a shallow stream, Lillian raised the cool water she had captured in her hands to her lips. The clear liquid slid down her parched throat, quenching the enormous thirst brought on by the sweltering late spring heat. After four hours of hard riding, Ethan had finally suggested they stop and rest the horses, refill the canteen, and eat a ration of the biscuits Emily had sent.

There had been no time for talking or seeking answers to the multitude of questions stacking up in her mind; just a desperate need to get as far away from Adela as they could in as little time as possible.

She splashed water on her face, then ran her moist hands down her throat and around her nape, where several damp strands of hair clung to her sticky skin. She had no idea where they were or where they were going; she was only glad that she was with Ethan. For now, that was enough.

She was drying her face with the skirt of her green calico dress when a feathery sensation brushed the back of her neck and she sensed someone was watching her. Twisting her upper body around, she found Ethan walking toward her, the canteen dangling from his hand, his face a mask of intense emotion she couldn't define.

He crouched beside her, uncapping the canteen. "How are you doing?"

She was a bit tired and becoming aware of muscles she didn't know existed, but determined not to complain. "I'm doing fine," she said, offering him a smile.

Without responding, he leaned forward and dipped the canteen into the gentle flow of the stream.

Lillian knew he was a man of few words, but shortly after they left Thomas and his associates that morning, Ethan had fallen into a pensive silence. She could feel him withdrawing from her, shutting her out of his every thought, forbidding her to touch even the smallest of his emotions.

She wanted to help, and wished, in many ways, God had made her Cherokee so she could share Ethan's pain, feel his grief, and help carry his burden. And she wished it didn't hurt so much that he refused to let her try.

She wiped her palms on her skirt. He may view her as an outsider, but there were a few things she had a right to know. "Where are we going?"

He capped the canteen. "We're going to a place called The Blue Haven. It's about eighty miles north of here. Very few white men know of its existence." He hesitated a contemplative moment. "Some of my people are already there; those who, like my family, chose to defy the removal treaty and remain in the land of our ancestors."

Surprise washed over Lillian. "You mean, you've been planning to flee all along?"

"Yes."

A twinge of disappointment needled through her. When she had come to him yesterday and told him about the troops and her father's part in the removal, why hadn't he told her that he and his family would not be there when the treaty enforcement took place? Did he not trust her?

"Where are Emily and the children?" she asked.

"We'll catch up with them tonight, at a place called Eagle's Nest."

An unsettling thought drifted into her mind. "What if the troops find you?"

"It's a risk we're willing to take." He slipped the canteen strap over his shoulder. "The next hour or so we'll be traveling over rough terrain. You'll ride with me."

Earlier, Ethan had released two of the outlaws' horses near a camp of Cherokee who had been driven from their home by intruders. Lillian now rode Thomas's buckskin mare, which had actually been stolen from Ethan's stock several months ago while his horses were grazing outside the corral.

"Are you saying my riding skills are lacking?" she said in jest, hoping to lighten the forlorn mood.

An ominous scowl marred Ethan's forehead. "The situation we find ourselves in is nothing to joke about."

The lighthearted expression she had pasted on her face withered. "I was only trying to help—"

"It doesn't help to make light of a family having to flee their home."

She clenched her teeth. He wasn't the only one who had fled today—and she had left her family behind. "Well, it doesn't help to brood either." Temper flaring, she bent forward, cupped her hand in the river, and threw a palm full of water in his face. Then she scrambled up and stormed away to join Billy and the horses, a bit surprised that Ethan hadn't grabbed her and bent her over his knee.

Heaven help her, her temper was her greatest weakness.

&

Ethan remained kneeling beside the stream, cool droplets of water streaming down his face and neck. She had retaliated to his harsh words then stalked away like an angry hen. But the image of her lovely face, brimming with both fury and hurt, lingered in front of him, vividly reminding him he had one more battle to fight—his toughest one yet.

No matter what he tried, he could not distance himself from her. With her passionate spirit and unbending loyalty, she wouldn't let him. He scrubbed a weary hand down his face. How could he bear to see her suffer? And she surely would in days to come.

And when the time came, how could he bear to let her go?

&

When Ethan joined Billy and Lillian, he made no mention of her temper tantrum. He simply ate a biscuit, then started to transfer his surplus saddle equipment to her mount.

Stepping up next to him, Lillian ran a hand down the mare's sleek neck. "The horse is trained so well, Ethan, I think she and I together can handle the rough terrain."

He continued tying his bedroll to the buckskin's saddle.

"Lillian, you're a good rider, but frolicking about a plantation can't be compared to this mountain terrain."

His words stung. She turned her back on him to hide her hurt. Why all the hostility? Was he angry that she was there? Holding on to the bridle with one hand, she rubbed the horse's nose with the other. The decision to come had had to be made without forethought. But, even if she had not wanted to, she couldn't let Ethan and Billy kill Thomas and his partners this morning without trying to intervene, even if it meant she could return to Adela without fearing for her life.

She held out her palm, allowing the mare to sniff. At the time, she had thought she made the right decision. Now, she wasn't so sure. She was beginning to feel she was in the way; extra baggage weighing Ethan down. Perhaps she should have insisted on returning to Adela. She could have made it to her father's camp long before Thomas found a way out of the forest without "exposing" himself. She would have been safe at the post. And when her father learned of Thomas's involvement in the pony clubs, he would have seen that justice was served. . .or, at least, attempted to.

But standing there this morning, faced with a decision that would determine the course of the rest of her life, all she could see was where she wanted to be—with Ethan.

Releasing the bridle, she brushed her hands on the skirt of her dress, feeling more out of place by the minute. It was becoming clear to her that Ethan didn't want the same thing she did.

She felt the gentle pressure of his hand on her shoulder and closed her eyes. Could she have been wrong about what his touch told her? Was she wrong in what she thought it was telling her now? That he did care—deeply?

Slowly, he turned her to face him. When she opened her eyes and looked up at him, what she saw in his face clogged her throat with emotion. The cold, hard edge was gone. In its place were the familiar, unspoken words of affection that told her the inextricable bond between them was real, not imagined.

He settled both hands on her shoulders. "Lillian, I didn't mean to be critical. But you must understand, these mountains are full of hidden burrows and crevices, and sharp rocks covered by dense undergrowth. One wrong step, and a horse could go down, taking the rider with it."

"And what if your horse is the one that goes down?"

"He won't."

The assuredness in his voice left no room for further argument. She turned to Black Thunder to help transfer Ethan's extra saddle equipment to her horse. But Billy had already taken care of the task and was sitting astride his own mount.

When Ethan and Lillian looked up at the handsome young man, he shook his head and grinned. "We'd better get moving, unless you two lovebirds want to become jailbirds."

They rode up, down, and through places Lillian thought too rugged for even the wildest of animals to travel, much less horses and human beings. Once again, Ethan spoke to Lillian through his touch. He embraced her waist to keep her steady in the saddle. He extended a hand to sweep aside branches that would have hit her in the face. He bent over her, covering her head with his arm, when they rode under low tree limbs.

At times, when the journey became less rugged, he didn't suggest she return to her mount, and neither did she. She simply sat astride Black Thunder in the circle of Ethan's strong arms until they stopped again to rest the horses.

Just before sundown, Ethan reined in his horse near the edge of a small clearing. Across the open area, a steep mountain rose until it seemed to touch the sky.

With intense concentration, Ethan and Billy scanned their surroundings. After perusing to his satisfaction, Ethan cupped his hands over his mouth and mimicked a birdcall. Emily broke through the wall of trees and dense foliage on the other side of the clearing and rushed toward them, a huge smile on her face. Ethan slid from his horse just in time to catch her as she threw her arms around his neck.

When Emily moved on to Billy, Ethan reached up to help Lillian dismount. All else faded into the distant background.

With their gazes locked, he gently lifted her to the ground. The heartrending tenderness in his eyes almost overwhelmed her. But, looking deeper, she saw a poignant sadness that sent a foreboding chill down her spine. Where would their road lead? Wherever that was, Lillian sensed that Ethan thought the journey would not be a long one.

He brushed an errant strand of hair away from her face. "Later, we'll talk."

She nodded, and he stepped back, dropping his hands from her waist. Her palms fluttered away from his chest.

Emily stepped forward, her hands stretched out in greeting, her eyes shimmering with joyous tears. "I'm so happy my brothers found you in time. Our provisions are meager, but whatever we have, we want you to consider yours."

Emily's sincere welcome moved Lillian. She may not be among family, but she was among friends.

Volunteering to see to the horses, Billy gathered the reins and took off toward one end of the thicket across the clearing. Ethan and Lillian followed Emily to the same dense wall of trees, mountain laurel, honeysuckle, and ferns.

Ethan parted the branches, then stepped back to allow Lillian to precede him. "When you go through a thicket, watch the limbs and try not to bend or break them," he explained. "And always try to cover your tracks."

Nodding, Lillian gathered up the folds of her dress and ducked into the thicket. When she stepped through to the other side, she found herself inside the cool, dank hollow of a cave. In awe, she scanned her surroundings. Several burning candles protected by sconces sat around the stone floor, throwing a pleasant yellow light over the rugged cavern walls and reflecting off the damp rock like moonbeams on a lake. A small stockpile of supplies sat to one side. In the center of the candlelight, Ethan's second cousin, Jim, his nine- and ten-year-old sons, and Ethan's nephew and niece sat on a blanket playing some sort of game with butter beans.

When the children spied Ethan, they abandoned their game and rushed toward him. Kneeling on one knee, Ethan stretched out his arms. All four youngsters somehow managed to find a place within his wide embrace.

Lillian watched, a warm smile curving her lips, until a movement in her outer field of vision drew her attention. She turned her head as someone stepped from the shadows. Slowly, her smile faded and her eyes rounded with shock. "Uncle Frederick?"

The tall, lanky man stepped up to her, his big shadow swallowing her as he approached.

Her breathing grew labored. Why was he here? Had he come to take her home? Were there others waiting outside? What did this mean for Ethan and his family?

Frederick stopped in front of her, his expression concealed by the shadows. "Lillian," he rasped, then gathered her in his arms.

Her mind reeling between fear for Ethan and his family and bewilderment, Lillian hugged him back. "Uncle Frederick, I didn't expect to find you here."

After a few seconds, he drew back, allowing his hands to settle on her upper arms. "Jim sent word to me this morning after Ethan and Billy left to find you. I had to come. I had to make sure you were all right." Pausing, he touched her face. "You are, aren't you? Those monsters didn't hurt you, did they?"

Lillian blinked. Obviously, he didn't know one of those "monsters" was his son—and she wasn't prepared to tell him. "I'm fine." She forced a smile. "Ethan and Billy arrived just in time."

Frederick turned his attention to Ethan, who had finished greeting the children and now stood beside her. "You and Billy. Are you both all right?"

"Yes."

Frederick and Ethan grasped each other's right forearm, close to the elbow. An Indian version of a handshake, Lillian assumed.

"I know you did it because you're an honorable man, and not out of any obligation to me," the older man said. "But I'll never be able to thank you enough for going after my niece."

Ethan sent Lillian a glance that spawned a fluttery sensation beneath her ribs. "I'm just thankful we got there in time," he said.

Next, Jim Walker greeted Lillian. A pleasant-natured man, Lillian guessed he was in his late thirties. He favored Ethan, but Jim wore his hair shorter, had dark, obsidian eyes, and stood a couple of inches shorter than his second cousin. He welcomed Lillian with as much sincerity as Emily had.

An overwhelming sense of acceptance filled Lillian with awe and wonder. How could a people who had suffered years of mounting oppression, seen countless loved ones unjustly persecuted, and been forced to leave their homes still offer an outsider such amicable hospitality?

When Jim drew Ethan away for a private conversation, Lillian turned to Frederick. "You knew, didn't you?"

"That Ethan and his family were planning to leave? Yes."

"You helped them," she guessed. "That's what all those late-night meetings were about, weren't they?"

He nodded.

Little by little, things were beginning to fall into place. Her uncle, like an angel of mercy, had been helping the Cherokee in secret, providing them a place to live, and helping them plan their escape. Thank God, there were a few people like him left.

She had many more questions she wanted to ask Frederick, but refrained in lieu of another inquiry preying on her mind. "Did you see Papa before you left?"

Sympathy mellowed his worry-worn features. "No, Lillian. To tell your father I know where you are would put Ethan and his family in danger. I figured it best just to let things unfold as they would if I didn't know."

What Frederick said was true. If her father found out the Walkers' whereabouts, he'd be duty-bound to apprehend them and take them back to Adela. Thomas and his partners would fabricate a story against Ethan and Billy, and the two would be arrested, possibly hanged.

Tears stung her eyes, burned the back of her throat. Would she ever see her father again?

"Lillian, I can't take you back to Adela now without arousing suspicion. When things settle down, I'll find a way to get you back to your father. Then I'll beg his forgiveness. But for now, we don't have any choice."

"I can't go back." Thomas would surely be back in town, spreading lies about her disappearance. She couldn't risk running into him.

"Can't, or don't want to?"

She shifted her gaze to Ethan, standing with his arms crossed, feet braced shoulder-width apart, still in deep conversation with Jim. Today she'd been forced to make a critical decision without the opportunity to stop and consider the consequences. If she had the chance to do it all over again, knowing what she knew now—all she would have to give up—would she make the same choice again?

As though sensing her gaze upon him, Ethan glanced her way, smiled, and then turned his attention back to Jim.

Lillian's heart overflowed with love. Yes, the decision would have been the same.

Looking up at Frederick, she answered his question the only way she could. "Both."

nine

Ethan lay on his bedroll near the cave entrance, staring up at the dark cavern ceiling and listening to Lillian's restlessness. She had probably never slept on the ground before, and certainly not in a cave.

Laying his forearm across his forehead, he closed his eyes, wishing he could change fate. He wanted so much for her: to marry her, give her a proper home, dress her in satin and lace, and lay her down on a soft feather bed. He longed to give her all the things she was accustomed to, all the things she deserved. But he couldn't; not for a very long time. Perhaps never.

And that made the cursed removal twice as painful as it had been two months ago. He had not only lost his home and his life's work. Eventually, he would lose Lillian, too.

His own restlessness stirred. How was he going to handle his feelings for her until that time came? How was he going to stay away from her?

He heard her release a disgruntled sigh. Opening his eyes, he looked toward the area where she, Emily, and the children had bedded down fifty or so feet deeper into the cavern. In the dim light of a few candles they had left burning, she threw back her cover, got up, and reached for her satchel. She had been so happy when she discovered that he and Billy had retrieved the bag from the woods. The first thing she had done was ask about her Bible.

Satchel in hand, she picked up a glowing sconce and crept toward the back of the cave, her waist-length hair shimmering down her back like a moonbeam. She disappeared around a bend in the cavern wall.

Ethan released a weary breath. What was she up to now? Grabbing a blanket, he got up and followed. He found her sitting, her legs crisscrossed, her back near the cave wall. The candle stood on the ground close to one knee. She was opening her Bible in her lap.

"You'll catch your death of a chill sitting on that cold ground," he told her.

She looked up, her exquisite features softening with a welcoming smile. "Did I disturb you?"

Yes, he was tempted to say. Every time he looked at her, smelled her, touched her, even thought of her, she disturbed him. "No," he answered. "I couldn't sleep."

"Neither could I."

She stood, holding the candle, satchel, and Bible while he spread the blanket on the stone floor. When she sat back down, she held her testament in her lap with her finger marking her place, but didn't reopen the book.

He stood, hesitating. Should he join her? Or leave her alone to read her Bible?

She gazed up at him, her expression inviting, and swept aside the billowy folds of her dress.

He needed no further prompting. He sat down, one leg outstretched, the other bent, and leaned back against the cave wall.

She glanced around the raw stillness that surrounded them, her eyes searching the craggy rock formation above and the obscure shadows beyond the candle's yellow glow. "I've never been inside a cave before. It's hard to believe it's so cold in here when it's so warm outside."

"With no sunlight to penetrate the darkness, the rock walls never get warm," he explained. "It's this way even during the hottest months of summer."

"Like the hearts of people," she mumbled under her breath.

"What was that?" he asked, wondering if he'd heard her correctly.

She blinked, as if his question jerked her out of a daydream, and looked up at him. "Oh, I was just thinking about something Uncle Frederick said during one of his sermons."

"And what was that?"

"He said, 'A person's heart is like the stony walls of a cold, dark cave until he or she allows the Light of God inside.' "

Something unsettling swept through Ethan; a disturbing and foreboding sensation he had experienced more than once over the past few weeks. It always left his heart pounding and his chest feeling heavy and hollow at the same time. He drew up his outstretched leg and straightened the other. "Do you read your Bible often?" he asked, hoping to lead into a pleasant conversation and dispel his disconcerting thoughts.

"I try to read at least a chapter a day. More when I'm restless or troubled. . . . It gives me peace."

Peace, Ethan repeated in his mind. That was something he had not felt for a very long time. Seventeen years, to be exact.

He studied her face, noticing a trace of trepidation. "Are you troubled now, Lillian?"

She paused a moment before answering. "I'm worried about what's going to happen. . .to all of us. And concerned my presence is going to make the journey harder for you and your family. But I'm not sorry I'm here."

Finally, he could ask the question he'd been waiting to ask all day. "Why, Lillian, do you even want to be here?"

She ducked her head, focusing on the Bible she still held in her lap. "Do you even need to ask?"

No, he didn't. She was there for the same reason he would have to someday let her go.

He could say the words. They were right there, on the surface of his tongue. But to tell her he loved her would be offering false hope. . .and promises he couldn't keep.

He allowed at least ten seconds to pass while he steeled himself with the courage to say what needed to be said. For her, he reminded himself. He was doing it for her. "Lillian, you and I. . .*us.* It can never be."

Calmly, she raised her head and looked at him, her placid expression telling him she did not agree. "Why?" Her silken voice was soft and unwavering.

He forced his gaze to remain steady on hers, even though he was tempted to gather her in his embrace and tell her everything would be all right; that staying with him would not mean suffering, and hardship, and leaving behind the life she was accustomed to. But he couldn't, not in truth. "Now it is my turn to say, 'Do you even need to ask?'"

"Yes, I do."

"Look around you." He made a wide sweep with his hand. "We're in a cave with nothing but the cold, hard ground to sleep on. Our food is limited to dried meat and stale bread because we can't build a fire to cook over. By now, everyone in Adela, including your father, thinks I kidnapped you. When we leave, we'll be looking over our shoulders." He pressed a fist to his chest. "Not only am *I* a fugitive, Lillian. By defying the treaty, my entire family and many of my people have become fugitives."

"Only in the eyes of some men, Ethan. Not in my eyes, and not in the eyes of God."

Elbow on bent knee, Ethan propped his forehead on the heel of his hand and funneled his fingers through his hair. She had an answer for everything. What would she say if he told her that, in the eyes of God, he was worse than a fugitive? He was a sinner, bound for hell, with a heart just as cold, dark, and stony as the walls of this cave.

He closed his eyes, once again trying to force his thundering heart to calm. What was wrong with him? Was he ill? Was his heart sick with some kind of deadly disease?

The thought struck him like a hurtling arrow. What if he were to die? What then? A sharp and agonizing fear gripped him. He would be forever separated from Emily, Billy, and Jim, for they all believed in God, and Jim and Emily were teaching their children to do the same.

He would be eternally separated from Lillian, the woman he loved more than his own life.

But, above all, he would be separated from God.

Ethan realized that, for the first time in his life, he was afraid to die.

Someone touched his arm. Startled, he looked up and stared blankly into Lillian's worried face. For one harrowing moment, he had forgotten she was there. Had forgotten everything. . .except that he was lost.

"Are you all right?" she asked, her voice reverberating with concern.

"Yes," he lied.

He could tell by the troubled frown creasing her brow that she was not convinced.

"Excuse me," he said. "I need to be alone for a while. Don't go any deeper into the cave. You could get lost." With that, he got up and walked away, hoping she would not follow. What he needed to sort out was between him and God—the God who had deserted Ethan and his mother seventeen years ago.

❧

Lillian watched Ethan disappear around the bend of the cavern wall. Something was wrong. Something that went beyond the removal, or the fact that he and his family had been forced to flee their home and hide out in a cave.

Something that was keeping him from God.

Lillian had first noticed it the day he pulled her from the Chestatee River. Every time she or anyone else referred to their faith, he would glance away, withdraw from the conversation, and erect a wall that kept everyone outside his emotions.

Jim, Emily, and Billy all believed, and were open and forthright about their faith. Ethan was raised in the same household, surrounded by the same values. What made him so indifferent to Christianity when the rest of his family was so passionate about theirs? Had something happened in his life to turn him away from God?

Her shoulders rose and fell on a dejected sigh. She wished she could help, but he'd made it clear he wanted to be alone. Besides, what could she do when there was so much of himself he refused to share with her?

Her gaze slid to the Bible, and she was reminded of one thing she could do. The same thing she'd been doing for Ethan and his people since she'd first met him. Hugging the treasured book to her chest, she bowed her head and began to pray.

Ethan made his way outside. After the dank chilliness of the cave, the night air hung thick and heavy, almost smothering him. Or was it the battle between good and evil bearing down upon his lungs?

He looked up at the dome of dark blue velvet sprinkled with countless points of light. A crescent moon hovered high in the sky. A misty cloud, like a translucent, white ghost, stretched her vaporous body across the center of the endless expanse.

Somewhere on a distant mountaintop, a coyote howled. Then, as if rebuking a bad omen, a dove cooed.

"How, God?" Ethan asked barely above a whisper. "If You are really there, if You really exist, how can I know for sure? And how can You save someone like me? My sins are so many, my thoughts have been so evil."

A twig snapped. Ethan whipped his head around, his eyes trained on the shadowed area from where the sound had come. Every nerve in his body hastened to alert; then he realized he had forgotten his gun. How could he have been so stupid?

"Relax, Ethan, it's just me." Frederick Price stepped quietly from the shadows, a rifle resting in the crook of one arm.

The tension seeped from Ethan's body. He had forgotten Frederick was taking first watch tonight. Ethan's shoulders dropped another begrudging inch. He seemed to be forgetting a lot of things all at once.

Frederick sidled up and stood next to Ethan. "I thought Jim was going to take the second watch."

"He is. I was just restless and needed some fresh air."

"If you can call this fresh," Frederick replied flatly. His gaze roamed the silhouetted treetops. "If the heat and lack of rain are a sign of what the summer will be like, I fear the journey west will be torturous for your people."

It would, Ethan had to silently agree. Traveling west in sweltering heat or hiding out in the woods and living off roots and berries, either way, the Cherokee had lost. . .everything.

"I'm worried about Lillian," Ethan said. "How do you think she will fare until I can get her back to Virginia, or to her father?"

"Lillian has a strong spirit and a lot of determination. She also has an unwavering faith in God. She will do fine."

Faith in God. Did it really help? Ethan wondered. What could it offer when one was facing a life of uncertainty? When all hope was gone? When one's fate was sealed?

Peace.

The word came to Ethan like a beacon of light penetrating the darkest hour of midnight. Was it possible to find peace in the midst of the chaos and confusion raging all around him? To find hope in a tomorrow that looked so dim?

A fierce desperation to know rose within him, giving him the courage to seek the answer. "Frederick, Lillian told me that when she is troubled, reading her Bible gives her peace. How can that be with all that has happened to her today? All that she is facing tomorrow? And for days to come?"

Frederick allowed a thoughtful silence to pass. "Sometimes, Ethan, one must look within himself to find peace."

"How does one do that?"

"By praying and humbling yourself before God with thanksgiving."

A swift surge of anger tore through Ethan. "What do *I* have to be thankful for?"

"You're alive," Frederick said without hesitation. "You have your strength and your health. Most of your family is with you; the rest is waiting for you in your new home. You have food and shelter. . . . Lillian is alive and here with you." The last he added in a low voice full of perception.

He paused, giving Ethan a chance to consider all that provident preparation had provided. Ethan and his family had taken the New Echota treaty ratification seriously, so they had prepared by finding an unexplored place in which to make a new home, mapping out a flight trail, and laying up provisions along the way.

But what about Lillian being there? That hadn't been in Ethan's plans.

Had it been in God's?

Ethan thought back over the day's events. What if Lillian

hadn't reached Tralyta before those vile men could violate her? What if Ethan and Billy hadn't found Lillian before Thomas had thrown her off the cliff? Ethan would have killed the three pony club members without batting an eye, and his own brother could have hanged alongside him for it.

He rubbed the back of his neck. What had determined the timing of each event, when less than a minute more would have resulted in disaster? Divine intervention? Could God have been working in Ethan's life, even then?

"You have more than many of your people have, Ethan," the minister added, pulling Ethan away from his ponderous thoughts.

"They knew the removal was coming," Ethan responded, his voice flat. "They could have been prepared."

"True," Frederick agreed. "We tried to warn as many as we could, but they would not listen. Now, it's too late."

Too late, Ethan repeated in his mind. He had prepared for the removal, but what preparations had he made for his soul?

None.

Was it too late? Ethan had distanced himself so far from God; would He even want anything to do with Ethan now?

The thought sent a chill of despair racing down Ethan's spine. He had to at least try to reach God. But first, he had to know how.

"Instructions on finding this peace. . . Are they in your Bible?"

"Yes. Philippians, chapter four, verses six and seven. 'Be careful for nothing; but in every thing by prayer and supplication with thanksgiving let your requests be made known unto God. And the peace of God, which passeth all understanding, shall keep your hearts and minds through Christ Jesus.' Any child of God who does that with a humble heart has the promise of peace."

"How does one become a child of God?"

"Romans, chapter ten, verse nine. 'That if thou shalt confess with thy mouth the Lord Jesus, and shalt believe in thine heart that God hath raised him from the dead, thou shalt be saved.'"

Ethan considered what Frederick was saying, turned each passage of Scripture over in his mind. "How does one know when it happens?"

"You feel it right here." Frederick tapped Ethan's chest. " 'A new heart also will I give you, and a new spirit will I put within you: and I will take away the stony heart out of your flesh, and I will give you an heart of flesh.' Ezekiel, chapter thirty-six, verse twenty-six."

Ethan released a pensive breath. "It all sounds so. . .simple."

"It is. All it takes is a willing heart."

Swiftly, the pounding rose again in Ethan's chest, thundered in his ears, sent waves of anticipation rolling through his body. Then, like lightning splitting a storm-darkened sky, the revelation came to him. It was true. God was real. The pounding heart and sudden fear of death was the voice of God calling, bidding Ethan to come and be saved.

"Would you like for me to pray with you?" Frederick asked, penetrating Ethan's stirring thoughts.

Ethan looked at the minister through the thick layer of night. "Thank you, Frederick. But this is something I need to do alone."

The preacher nodded. "I understand."

Ethan walked away, entering the shelter of the dense forest. Some people may find comfort in the presence of others when they are seeking redemption, but Ethan wanted solitude. He didn't want to be distracted by the voice of another speaking on his behalf, looking on in expectation, or laying hands on his pulsing skin. He wanted no one present, except him and God.

He weaved around towering trees, lumbered over rotting stumps, and clawed through clinging branches until he stepped out of the woods onto the narrow shore of a secluded mountain lake. The water's surface was calm and as smooth as glass. A thin sliver of moonlight and myriad points of starlight glittered on the plane of water. The air reverberated with the katydids' rhythmic cadence and a frog's swelling groan.

Ethan stared at the placid lake and thought back over his

life, his many sins and iniquities. He had taken the Lord's name in vain, a few times tried to find solace in strong drink, hated his enemy, and lain with women to satisfy a need with no thought or promise of commitment.

There were many more—too many to name. But God knew them all, and only He had the power to forgive them and grant Ethan the pardon he so desperately needed.

His throat began to ache. His eyes burned. The points of light reflecting off the lake crystallized. "Oh, God, my God," Ethan whispered. "Please have mercy on me, a sinner."

A shiver tightened Ethan's scalp, then flowed down his body and throughout each limb. His legs gave way, and he fell to his knees. Covering his damp eyes with his hands, he bowed his face to the ground.

Desire filled his soul, and a flash of light warmed the cold, dark hollow in the center of his chest, severing the strings to a heart of stone.

His shoulders shook, his body trembled, and from the deep recesses of his mind, a beautiful vision sprang forth—nail-scarred hand reaching out to him.

Tears streaming, heart willing, Ethan sat back on his heels and lifted his eyes and hands toward heaven.

❧

The sun peeked over the rolling blue horizon, adding a touch of gold to the marbled pink eastern sky. A soft and gentle breeze stirred the trees. Birds greeted the new day with song.

Ethan stood waist-deep in the lake's water. Beside him stood his friend, Reverend Frederick Price. Lined up on the shore were Ethan's family and Lillian. They had taken a risk by all leaving the shelter of the cave at once. But when Ethan asked Frederick to baptize him before they continued their journey, no one would be deterred from making the short trip to the lake to see him christened into the family of God. Ethan knew Jim, Emily, and Billy had prayed for this for a long time. From the stream of tears flowing down Lillian's face, Ethan suspected she had sent up a few prayers of her own.

He scanned the onlookers. Just yesterday, he would have

shaken his head and wondered what all of the fuss was about. Today, he understood the importance of a family being united in Christ, of knowing that separation from loved ones in this life did not mean separation for good.

"Are you ready?" Frederick asked.

Ethan nodded.

Laying one hand on Ethan's shoulder and raising the other heavenward, the preacher repeated a traditional baptismal recitation. "Upon obedience and command of our Lord and Savior, and upon his profession of faith in Christ, I baptize thee my brother, in the name of the Father, and of the Son, and of the Holy Ghost."

Frederick moved one hand to Ethan's back, the other to his chest, and dipped Ethan into the cool water. Ethan emerged, hands raised in praise and worship to his new Savior, and feeling like his soul had been cleansed a second time.

After he stepped out of the water onto the shore, Frederick and each family member, including the children, took turns embracing Ethan and expressing their joy over his salvation. When everyone else had wandered away, there stood Lillian, an exquisite creature in the brilliance of the rising sun. Her eyes were now dry and her face radiant.

Ethan's chest tightened. Oh, how bittersweet this moment. They were now united in Christ, but they would never be united as man and wife. That much had not changed.

Slowly, she stepped forward, stopping with less than a foot between them. Her balmy scent filled his head. Her warm presence chased the lingering chill of the lake from his body. And the way she looked at him, with reverence and open adoration, made him feel he could do anything—even give her the kind of life she deserved. Apparently, salvation didn't make him any less of a flesh-and-blood man.

His throat tightened with amorous emotion. He started to raise an empty palm to her face, but a needle of warning pricked his conscience. He forced his hand to stay by his side and guided his thoughts in another direction. "You knew, didn't you?" he said.

She nodded. "Ever since the day you rescued me from the river, I suspected something was wrong. I wasn't sure what until last night. Just that it had something to do with your relationship with God." Rising up on her toes, she circled his neck with her arms and laid her head against the damp shirt covering his chest.

His arms, with a sudden will of their own, slipped around her. One hand tunneled beneath her silky hair and found the middle of her back, the other cupped the back of her head. Her small, shapely body felt like a beautiful dream wrapped inside his arms—one he wanted to hold on to forever. A painful shudder of longing raked through him, and he closed his eyes. *Why, Lord? If we can't be together, why do we love each other this way?*

Too soon, she withdrew her arms from around his neck and lowered her heels to the ground, but she didn't pull away. He allowed his hands to rest on her slim waist.

Reaching up, she framed his face with her palms and looked deeply into his eyes. "I love you, Ethan Walker."

Her soft-spoken confession rocked Ethan's world. His legs trembled, and his stomach quivered. His chest, he thought, would surely burst, for the words he had carried there so long fought for escape. Closing his eyes, he struggled to endure the war between desire and logic threatening to take away his breath. He loved her, too. More, even, than he had yesterday.

Too much to cause her great pain.

His last thought lent him the strength to temper his own needs and do what he knew was best for her. Opening his eyes, he reached up and pulled her hands away from his face, then he captured her upper arms and gently set her away from him. "I love you, too. . .my sister in Christ."

Her eyelids fluttered and, a heartbeat later, her serene expression melted into bewilderment, then withered into hurt.

Ethan's resolve weakened, but he somehow held it intact. She had to understand. They may love each other, but their worlds were too far apart.

She stepped back, forcing him to drop his hands from her

arms. The air surrounding him turned cold. Drawing back her shoulders, she lifted her chin a determined inch, revealing the resilient spirit he admired so much in her.

"I'm happy for you, Ethan," she said with only a slight tremor in her voice. "My constant prayer will be that God continues to bless you." Lifting the front of her dress a couple of inches, she turned and walked away, her attention now focused on the ground.

The dejected picture she made sliced through Ethan like a sharpened saber. One thing about a heart of flesh, the wounds cut more deeply than in one of stone.

ten

Frederick and Emily had waited for Lillian. Frederick stepped with her into the woods, but Emily marched up to Ethan, crossed her arms, and shifted her weight to one foot. Anger blazed in her dark eyes.

Ethan raked his wet hair away from his forehead. "What's wrong?"

"What did you say to Lillian?" she asked, her voice ladened with reproach.

"That's between Lillian and me."

"Now it is between you and me."

"No, it isn't. I won't discuss it with you." He started to step around her.

She blocked his path, pressing a hand to his chest. "Fine. You can listen to what I have to say. Then, if you still want to let the second-best thing that's ever happened to you walk out of your life, you'll have only yourself to blame while you're sleeping on the hard ground alone for the next six months."

He didn't want to listen. He knew exactly what he'd just let walk away and didn't need his sister to remind him. But he knew she'd dog his every step until she had her say. "Talk," he said.

She drew in a deep breath and released it slowly. "I had Peter for six months."

A jolt of surprise straightened Ethan's shoulders. His sister never talked about her dead husband.

"Six months," she repeated more softly. Eyes misting, she focused on some unknown object to Ethan's right. "He didn't even get to see his children born."

She paused a moment to purse her quivering lips. "After he was gone, I thought I would die from grief for a very long time. Some days, I even wanted to die. But, you know what?"

115

She shifted her intense gaze back to Ethan's. "I'd go through it all again just to have one more day with him, to tell him and show him how much I loved him."

Ethan didn't have an immediate response. How could he argue with someone who had experienced the grief of losing the one she loved most? Lillian might not be dead when she left, but she would still be gone. "But Lillian is so different from us," he finally said, but the excuse didn't seem to hold as much merit as it once had. "She's used to having so much," he added, his voice lacking absolute conviction.

Emily shook her head. "Do you think that matters to her?"

"Perhaps not now, but—"

"Ethan, don't you have more faith in her than that? Or will your pride not allow you to accept that maybe you *don't* know what's best for everyone?" She paused, giving him a chance to consider her words.

"Put yourself in her place," Emily continued. "She loves you, just as much as you love her and in exactly the same way. Suppose you were the pampered rich man and she a peasant girl with only the ground to sleep on, and choosing her way of life was the only way you could be together. What would you be willing to give up?"

Everything slipped immediately into his mind.

Apparently his expression gave away his thoughts, for a look of satisfaction settled over Emily's face. She arched her dark brows. "Don't you think Lillian has the right to decide for herself what she wants?"

"But—"

"Don't think about tomorrow, Ethan," his sister said, intercepting what he was going to say. "None of us are assured we'll even get through this day."

Any further argument died on his tongue.

"You know God now, Ethan. It's time to get yourself out of the way, then you might see that Lillian is with us for a reason." With that, his sister turned and walked toward the trees.

"Wait." He trotted to catch up with her. "I'll walk with you." He didn't want her walking through the woods alone, even the short distance between the lake and Eagle's Nest.

Just before they reached the clearing in front of the cave, he grasped her arm, urging her to stop and face him. "Tell Frederick I'd like for him to postpone leaving for Adela for a few more minutes, if he can."

She studied him a perceptive moment, then a faint smile tipped her lips. "I will."

Emily stepped outside the trees, and Ethan turned and slipped deeper into the forest. He needed to find a private place to pray.

≈

Kneeling alongside Emily in front of a food crate, Lillian wrapped two pieces of corn bread and two pieces of dried meat in a small cloth. She was reluctant to accept the provisions Emily offered, but she and Frederick would need sustenance on the way back to Adela. At least, Frederick would. She doubted she'd ever be hungry again.

She tucked the victuals into her satchel. Ethan had finally said the words she so longed to hear, then squashed her hopes and dreams by adding "my sister in Christ."

Anger and anguish tumbled together inside her. She still sensed his feelings went deeper, but she couldn't stay knowing he was going to keep pushing her away. Rejection from her former fiancé had hurt. Ethan's rejection was breaking her heart. If he wanted to keep his distance from her, she'd make it easy for him. Perhaps, even, make it easier for them both.

So what if she had to do battle with Thomas? The way she felt right now, she could take on all the pony clubs.

"You should take a bedroll in case you and Frederick don't make it to Adela before dark," Emily said.

Not in the mood for conversation, Lillian nodded and pushed up off the hard floor.

With her back to the cave's mouth, she kneeled once again and started rolling up a blanket. She was tying a leather strap around the bedding when something alerted her attention. Pausing, she noticed dead silence surrounded her. Nothing stirred. Then a tingling awareness spread across her shoulders and she whipped her upper body around. Everyone was gone—except Ethan. And he was the last person she needed to see right now.

Ignoring the fluttering in her stomach, she turned her back on him and continued tying up the bedroll. She was working on the second string when his moccasin-covered feet, braced shoulder-width apart, appeared at her side.

"What are you doing?" he asked.

She refused to look up, but, in her mind's eye, she could see him, standing there with his arms crossed, looking down at her like she was a disobedient child.

Well, he need not concern himself with her activities much longer. "I'm packing. What does it look like I'm doing?" She gave the strap one final jerk. One side broke. She gritted her teeth. If she were a swearing woman, she'd be inclined to curse. She tossed the broken end of the strand aside. "I'm going back to Adela with Uncle Frederick."

"No, you're not."

That's what he thought. Arrogant man! At least she wouldn't have to listen to him telling her what she could and could not do anymore. She slapped a strand of hair back over her shoulder. Maybe leaving wouldn't be so hard, after all.

Even as the thought spilled into her mind, she knew it wasn't true. Leaving was killing her. She was dying inside, minute by agonizing minute.

Tucking the blanket under her arm, she scrambled up. When he grasped her upper arm to help her, her breath faltered. She stepped away from him, hoping he would take the hint and release her. He did.

She still couldn't look at him for fear she'd throw herself at him, pledge her undying love for him, and make an idiot out of herself—like she had at the lake. Glancing down, she pretended to brush the dust from her dirty dress. "Uncle Frederick will take me to my father's fort, and he will see that I get back to Virginia safely."

"Is that what you want?"

Stilling her motions, she closed her eyes and offered up a

quick request for courage. She didn't want Ethan to see how vulnerable she was to him. As she opened her eyes, she straightened her spine and looked up at him, leveling him with all the fortitude she could muster. "Obviously, Ethan, what I want doesn't matter."

His shadowed features softened. "Yes, Lillian, it does."

The knot in her stomach jumped up to her throat. She wanted to believe him. Oh, how she wanted to. But her feelings had never mattered to him before. They hadn't even mattered an hour go. Why would they now? "I'll be safe at the fort. There's really no reason for me to stay here." On wobbling legs, she walked to the food crate and picked up her satchel.

"Is this what I'm going to have to put up with for the rest of my life?"

She concentrated solely on slipping the bag's strap over her shoulder. "No, Ethan. After today, you'll never have to put up with it again." Looking straight ahead, she marched toward the cave's entrance. Three steps later, the words "for the rest of my life" caught up with her. She stopped, blinked, and then spun around to face him. "What did you say?"

With calm and confident deliberation, he strolled up to her. "I said: 'Is this what I'm going to have to put up with for the rest of my life?'"

"Wh—" She cleared her clogged throat. "What do you mean?"

An easy smile tipped his lips. "I mean, every time you get upset with me, are you going to pack up and threaten to run home to your father?" His smile remained, but the amusement left his eyes. A promise took its place. "Because, I'm warning you, once we're married, I won't let you go."

"M–married?"

&

She reminded Ethan of a startled hummingbird, about to come to her senses and take flight. He settled his hands on her shoulders, just in case. "Before we carry this conversation any further, there's something I want you to think about—how much your life will change if you become my wife."

"I already have," she answered quickly.

Too quickly, Ethan feared. He raised a skeptical brow. "Have you really?"

Her shoulders rose and fell on a slow, deep sigh. He sensed her struggling to calm herself, felt the delicate muscles beneath his hands begin to relax.

After a few poised seconds, a shadow of pain drifted across her face. "I know it will mean that I may not see my father again for a very long time. I've already considered that. As for the plantation. . ." A fierce and resolute light ignited her jade eyes, and she lifted her lovely chin a stubborn inch. "My home will be with my husband."

A strong and steady stream of peace flowed through Ethan, but faint traces of doubt still lingered. "Our life will be very different from the one you're accustomed to. There will be land to clear and homes to build. For months, we will have to bathe in streams, cook over an open fire. . .live in a thatched-roof shelter."

She made one small movement, and the blanket and satchel fell to the ground. Inching closer, she raised her hands and framed his face with her palms. "Ethan, our life together may be hard for a while; maybe even for a long time. There will always be prejudices, thieves, and cruel and unjust people. But we will face those hardships together, draw strength from each other, and find comfort in each other's arms. Otherwise, we will both be alone and empty, and life will be most miserable." Her expression mellowed. "At least, mine will. And not just for a week or a month or a year, but until I draw my last breath."

The loyalty and devotion in her countenance confirmed her words—and severed Ethan's last thread of doubt. He slid his hands from her shoulders, down her arms, and captured her hands. Then he dropped to one knee. "I love you, Lillian Gunter. Not only as my sister in Christ, but as a man loves a woman when he wants to make her his wife. Will you—"

"Yes," she said excitedly, breathlessly. The radiance in her face lit up the dim interior of the cavern.

Briefly, Ethan closed his eyes in relief. *Thank You, God.* Now, the next question was *When?* Opening his eyes, he said, "Frederick is right outside—"

"All right."

A slow smile spread across Ethan's face. Then, for the first time in a very long time, tides of laughter bubbled up from his chest. Standing, he wrapped his arms around his bride's waist, picked her up, and spun her around. The sounds of their joy echoed throughout the hollow of the cavern.

⁊⁊

Ten minutes later, Ethan and Lillian said their vows in the yellow candlelight reflecting off the cave's stone walls. Emily cried relentlessly, but not Lillian. There was no flowing white gown, no decorated church full of guests, and no father present to give her away. But there couldn't have been a lovelier bride. She literally glowed.

And Ethan, who had just lost almost all of his earthly possessions, stood by her side feeling like a rich man.

⁊⁊

Soon after the ceremony, Frederick said good-bye and headed outside. Jim accompanied the minister.

The arm draped around Lillian's shoulder tensed. As she glanced up at her husband, he met her gaze. "I'll be back in a minute," he said.

She read the look of dread on his face. "You're going to tell Uncle Frederick about Thomas, aren't you?"

Ethan nodded.

"Do you have to do it now?"

Remorse joined Ethan's dread. "Yes. Thomas must be stopped before he and his partners attack someone else."

"Do you honestly think Uncle Frederick will turn in his son?"

"I think he will pray about it, then do the right thing."

After only a few seconds' deliberation, Lillian had to agree. "Poor Uncle Frederick," she said on a despondent sigh. "He's going to be so disappointed."

❧

When Ethan told Frederick about his son, the preacher's eyes filled with sorrow, but not surprise.

The minister turned his gaze toward the craggy blue horizon. "I was afraid something was going on with Thomas. I saw the signs lately, but I just didn't want to believe it."

Ethan ached for his friend. "If you need to take some time before leaving, we can stay a while longer."

Looking back at Ethan, Frederick shook his head. "No. You need to get moving before someone looking for Lillian catches up with you." Shoulders hunched, he dropped his gaze to the ground. "Besides, I think I need to be alone for a while."

As he rode away, Jim said, "He reminds me a lot of David."

Confusion pinched Ethan's forehead. "Who?"

"King David, in the Bible. He was a man after God's own heart, but he had a son named Absalom who turned against him. For a time, Absalom even took over his father's throne."

Yes, Ethan thought, Frederick was a lot like David, and Thomas a lot like Absalom. Disgust settled in the pit of Ethan's stomach.

Greed. It was such an ugly monster.

eleven

That evening, Ethan sat cross-legged on the blanket he and his wife would sleep under, brushing her long, flaxen hair. Their "bedroom" was a small patch of earth within a wall of trees and mountain laurels, well secluded and hidden from the rest of the Walker family, but near enough to hear a cry for help or a warning of danger. Just a few feet away, the waters of a babbling brook danced over the rocks. The light of the half-moon bounced off the lively currents like countless diamonds sprinkled from heaven. A lone whippoorwill droned over the rhythmic song of the katydids.

Each brush stroke filled the air with the sweet-smelling herbs Lillian had used to wash her hair, but underneath the pleasant scent was the intoxicating, balmy fragrance that belonged to her alone.

He held his simmering emotions in check. He knew he could exercise his rights as a husband right now, and she would be willing. But would she be ready? The bashful way she had avoided his gaze and the nervous tremor in her hands when they'd spread their bedding had told him "No." That he should wait for the right time—for her. And that's exactly what he intended to do.

He funneled the fingers of his free hand through her thick tresses. The silken locks floated like a dream in moonlight over his skin. The shiny white and gold strands fell like a shimmering waterfall against the cream-colored gown she and Emily had fashioned out of meal sacks. In many ways, he was nervous, too. Yes, there had been women in his past, but none of such virtue as Lillian. And none who had planted such a need in him to do things right. Just knowing their union would be sanctioned by their love and God, and that when he rose and left their bed he wouldn't feel cheap and dirty as he had in days gone by, would make the reverent experience new and virtuous for him, too.

"Ethan?" Lillian said, her low, melodious voice interrupting his ponderous musings.

"Mmmm?"

"Tell me again about The Blue Haven."

"The Blue Haven," he repeated, for the first time looking forward to building a new house in a new land instead of resenting, so much, being forced to leave his old one. His new home would be governed by God, and made complete by Lillian, whether four solid walls surrounded them or not.

"The mountains there are high and the valley fertile," he said. "The streams are as clear as liquid crystal, and the lake is bountiful."

"How did you obtain this land? I mean, I thought our people weren't recognized as landowners."

Ethan grinned. He liked the way she referred to the Cherokee as "our" people, and not just his. "We're not. The land was recently purchased on our behalf in the name of a friendly white man."

"I see," she replied, but her tone told Ethan she really didn't.

Being a man who'd rather listen than speak, he wasn't fond of giving detailed explanations to anyone about anything. But she deserved to know exactly where her new life was taking her. So, for her, he decided to try.

"My great-grandfather, The Pathfinder, is chief of our clan. He believes we should strive for peace and friendship with the white people, but he protested fiercely the New Echota treaty. He feels we will be safer from aggression among the rocks and mountains, where the Great Spirit planted us, than the lands west of the Mississippi that the white man may someday find profitable and, in turn, remove us all over again.

"After the treaty was ratified two years ago, he gathered his people together and told us we needed to find a place of refuge and prepare for the day when the removal took place. Many of our clansmen didn't believe him and ignored his prophecy, thinking the removal would never really take place."

He paused a minute, thinking of those who hadn't listened, those who would soon be taken from their homes and locked in a stockade, like animals, then forced to make the grueling westward journey in the sweltering heat of summer. How many would survive?

"But a few of us—around one hundred—trusted my great-grandfather's instincts and began preparing," he continued. "Some of us searched out the Appalachian highlands and found The Blue Haven, which, you will see, is far removed from white civilization. My great-grandfather designated the valley as our City of Refuge during the removal, and we started raising the money to purchase the land."

"But you were going to be removed from the land in Georgia that's in Uncle Frederick's name," she injected. "What makes North Carolina so different?"

"For one thing, North Carolina is known for being a little more tolerant of our presence than Georgia. For another, the northern state has more places to hide. Our white friend, who secured the land, along with a few others like your uncle Frederick, is pushing Congress to allow us to stay on the lands being purchased on our behalf. Hopefully, that will happen soon. Until it does, the trick will be keeping our whereabouts a secret from anyone who might be a threat to our plans."

"Oh!" she said, like his long explanation finally made sense. "I really do see now." A few thoughtful seconds drifted by. "Ethan, may I ask you something?"

"You, my sweet wife, may ask me anything."

"This morning, at the lake, you. . .pushed me away."

He heard the strain of pain in her voice, and guilt pricked his conscience. He hadn't realized then how much his rejection had hurt her. "At the time, I thought I was protecting you."

"I know." There was no vanity in her voice, just the calm knowledge of his protective love. "But less than an hour later, you asked me to marry you. What happened between the lake and the cave to change your mind?"

He laid the brush aside and turned her around to face him. The knees of their crisscrossed legs touched. He grasped her hands and caressed the backs of her fingers with his thumbs. "Emily said some things to me that made me realize I had no right deciding what was best for you, and that I could be hurting you more by sending you away than by asking you to stay."

She sent him a smug I-tried-to-tell-you grin. "Your sister is a very wise woman."

He returned a sheepish smile. "Yes, she is." Then his smile faded. "I'm sorry I hurt you. I wish I could promise you that I'd never let anything hurt you again. But, I can't."

She withdrew one hand from his and pressed a cool palm to his cheek. "Just always love me, Ethan. That's all I ask."

"Asking me to love you is something you'll never have to do. I will always belong to you. *Always.*"

Her eyes were warm and trusting, her slightly-parted lips moist and inviting. Slipping his hand around her nape, he leaned forward, urging her to do the same. He brushed her pliant mouth with his. Her warm breath filled his head, igniting a spark inside him.

The next kiss was soft, sweet, and lingering, a symbol of innocence mingled with the promise of passion. She slipped her hand to the back of his head, tunneled her fingers through his hair. He angled his head, deepening the kiss. Her arm curled further around his neck. A smoldering ember jumped to life inside him. He rose to his knees and started to lay her down.

She stiffened.

Banking his rising desire, Ethan drew away and sat back down, once again gathering her hands in his.

She ducked her head. "I'm sorry."

He curled a forefinger beneath her chin, urging her to look at him. "It's all right, Lillian. Nothing has to happen until you're ready."

Her eyes misted. "I'm sorry," she repeated. "I don't mean to disappoint you."

His lips curved in understanding. "I love you, *aquatseli Liliyani,* you could never disappoint me."

A tear escaped and trickled down her cheek. He captured

the droplet with his thumb, then gathered her in his embrace and pulled her onto his lap. She came willingly, wrapping her arms around his shoulders and burying her face in his neck. In spite of her gentle weeping, the smile lingered on his lips. Wedding night timidity. Thank goodness, Emily had warned him. An overwhelming sense of protection spread throughout his entire being. He tightened his arms around her.

Silently, she cried while he rocked her back and forth, kissed her temple, caressed her hair, comforted her in every way he could. When her tears ebbed, she drew back and wiped her cheeks with her hands. As he brushed a clinging strand of hair away from her damp face, she drew in a deep, shuddery breath. "I love you," she whispered.

"And that's enough."

An amazing sense of contentment stole over Ethan, and he knew it was true. The husband-wife union did not complete a marriage. It was love, trust, loyalty, and a willingness to give more than receive. Those things sealed the marriage bond more than the union did. Without one, the other meant nothing, but love was the foundation for it all. And as long as he had Lillian's, he would be there for her, with her, completing her that same way she completed him. The rest, he knew, would come in its own time.

"It's getting late," he said. "Why don't we lie down?"

She nodded, and Ethan sensed she knew that's all he was asking of her. Just to lay beside him and allow him to hold her.

He laid back on the blanket covering the thin layer of leaves he'd gathered that evening, then opened his arms, giving her a soft place to rest. When she settled, he pulled up the top blanket, then wrapped her in his embrace. She fit perfectly in the crook of his arm.

Satisfied and content, Ethan closed his eyes and offered up a silent prayer of thanksgiving. Before long, the first stages of sleep began to claim his mind.

"Ethan?"

His wife's velvety voice pulled him back from the brink of oblivion. "What?"

"Did I wake you?"

"No." He tried to rub his eyes on the sly, but she twisted around to her side and saw him.

"Liar," she said, her tone laced with mirth.

"Honest, you didn't. You caught me just in time." He blinked several times, then stretched his eyes wide. The moon offered just enough light for his gaze to connect with hers. "What did you want?"

"Nothing." She snuggled into his side. "Go back to sleep."

He tipped her chin, forcing her to look at him. "You wouldn't have called my name if you didn't have something you needed to say."

She studied him intently for a moment, then said, "What happened seventeen years ago?"

At first, he just stared at her, too caught off guard by her unanticipated question to react. Then a steadily mounting stream of dread pulsed through his veins.

As though sensing his rising disquietude, she flattened one palm against the center of his chest. "Emily mentioned it," she said, as though reading his next question as it evolved in his mind. "While we were preparing supper, she said today was the first time she'd heard you laugh in seventeen years. When I asked why, she said you should be the one to tell me." In the same breath, she added, "But, if you don't want to talk about it—"

Ethan pressed a finger to her lips, silencing her. No, he didn't want to talk about it, but he needed to. Lillian was his wife, and he wouldn't keep anything from her. He just hadn't planned on opening up to her about the one thing in his life he had never talked about—to anyone—on their wedding night.

She kissed his fingertip then pulled his hand away from her mouth, lacing her slim fingers through his. Her shadowed expression was supportive and undemanding.

Her calm patience gave him the courage he needed, but he tore his gaze away from her face and stared at the silhouetted trees above. Somehow it didn't seem appropriate to look at something so beautiful when talking about something so ugly.

There were details. Sickening details too repulsive for her to hear. *How much should I tell her, Lord?*

Only what she needs to hear.

Like the wind in a dying storm, a gradual calm edged out Ethan's disquietude. Then he forced his emotions into a state of paralyzing numbness, so he couldn't feel, so the wounds that had never healed would not break open and bleed profusely. "My mother used to attend to the sick and injured, like Emily does now. She would spend many spring days in the woods, collecting herbs. Sometimes I would go with her."

A tormenting memory flashed through his mind. He paused, waiting for it to fade. It dimmed, but didn't completely vanish. It never did.

"There weren't many intruders in our area then, and the few who were around didn't know our land was rich in gold. They kept their distance from us, as we did from them. We still felt safe scouring the woods for chestnuts or going across the river to visit our friends."

He swallowed to wet his parched throat. "One morning, while my mother and I were out gathering herbs, we came up on three men." Once, he would have said three "white" men. But he realized now it hadn't mattered what color their skin was, only what was in their hearts. That day, it had been evil. "They were moonshiners, operating an illegal whiskey still, and had been sampling their own brew."

The pressure of his wife's palm increased against his chest. He raised his hand to cover hers, drawing from her strength, her love. "They raped her," he finally said. And had made him watch every horrendous minute of it.

Shifting, Lillian raised up on her elbow. "Ethan, I'm so sorry."

He felt her peering down on him, eyes full of shock, sorrow, and pain. But he kept his gaze fixed on the black shadows of the trees. "Nine months later, Billy was born. I don't think my mother would have survived if it hadn't been for knowing she carried an innocent child inside her, depending on her life to sustain his."

"Billy is a wonderful young man," Lillian said, as though reaching for the only ray of light in the horrid story he was telling her.

"Yes," Ethan agreed, "he is." Finally, he looked at her, needing to feel the caring caress of her eyes while he admitted to the burden he'd carried since he was nine years old. "I couldn't do anything to help her, Lillian. Those men, they were too strong."

Lillian cupped his cheek with her palm. She bathed him in tenderness, compassion, and the one thing he needed most—understanding. "Ethan, you were just a little boy. There's probably nothing you could have done even if you had been a grown man." She shook her head. "It wasn't your fault."

He knew that now. And with God's grace, Lillian's love, and time, he'd learn to let go of the pain, and, somehow, get beyond the self-blame. "I stopped believing in God that day, Lillian. Stopped believing in all that is good and true and honest. I was a bitter and angry child who grew into a bitter and angry man. I've done things—"

She slid her fingers over his lips. "Those things don't matter anymore, Ethan. God took them all away when you asked Him to come into your life."

He kissed her fingertips, then pulled her hand away from his mouth. "We need to pray for my mother." Ethan had already told Lillian his mother was at The Blue Haven, waiting for them. She had been among the ones who went ahead to prepare for those that would follow. His father he never knew. The man whose face and name remained a mystery to Ethan had died before Ethan was born. "She was a Christian," Ethan added, "but she lost faith in God that day, too."

"We will, Ethan. God can help her let go of the past, just like He will help you."

"I know."

He took a moment to study her serene expression. She had been a Christian for ten years—half her life. He was a newborn, just beginning to taste the milk of life. Would he ever learn all he needed to know about following God? "There's so much I don't know, Lillian, about the Bible and being a Christian. Will you teach me?"

"What I can. But when it comes to the Bible, I'm just a student myself. There's always something new to learn, so many wonderful mysteries there, waiting to be discovered. It's a never ending process."

"Then we'll learn together."

Her lips tipped. "Yes, we will."

Like a floating satin cloak, a spellbinding stillness fell between them, and Lillian's smile faded. Their gazes met in a new and enrapturing way, and a silent message passed between them—one that spoke of love, trust, and promises kept.

Slowly, Lillian leaned over and pressed her soft, warm mouth to Ethan's. Her pale hair fell like a comforting blanket around him. Her alluring scent filled his head, awakening his senses, testing his resolve.

He lay there allowing her to kiss him, returning the affection, but taking only what she was willing to give. He didn't move, didn't breathe for fear he'd unleash the gently glowing fire she was stoking.

When she drew back, she brushed his lower lip with her fingertips, sending a sparkling tingle from his throat to his stomach, and looked at him with an intensity he could feel. He knew she'd never voice the words. At least, not this early in their marriage. But the message was there, in her trusting face.

He stroked her hair. "Are you sure?"

She nodded.

He raised up, cupping the back of her head in his hand, and eased her back onto the blanket.

"I love you, *Liliyani.*"

"I love you, too, Ethan."

As he lowered his head to claim her nectar-sweet lips, he tried to forget that the ground beneath them was hard and the ceiling above, a vast expanse of air and sky. Tried to forget the gown she wore was pieced-together meal sacks, and the bed she lay on was nothing but a thin blanket and a few leaves.

She deserved more. So much more. And if the Lord

allowed Ethan to live to see another year pass, he'd see that she had it.

Her arms rose to circle his neck. The fingers of one hand funneled through the hair at his nape. The fire inside Ethan began to grow.

He angled his head, tasting more. She was rain in the desert, honey in the wilderness, a healing touch that had brought him back from the brink of death.

Breath for breath, touch for touch, they both gave and received equally, both whispered silent promises in the moonlight.

Soon, the ceiling of sky and humble bed didn't matter, and the fact that he was a poor man with not even a shanty to offer his wife faded from his mind. For he became lost in the most beautiful experience he had ever known—the union of husband and wife.

twelve

Atop the peak of a steep incline, Lillian reined in her buckskin mare beside Ethan's black gelding. The rest of their family followed. They had been riding through thickly forested valleys and over rugged mountain terrain for close to six days now. For five nights, they had slept under the stars.

Lillian's weary body longed for a warm bath, a soft bed, and sleep. She knew the warm bath and soft bed were a dream for now. But, at the moment, she would gladly settle for a humble shelter, where she could lay her head on her husband's firm shoulder, feel his strong arms around her, and close her eyes without the fear of a snake or wild varmint crawling beneath the covers with them.

The journey had been grueling, unlike anything she had ever experienced. They'd bathed only once—in a frigid mountain stream—since leaving the cave, but Lillian's dress had known no such luxury. It reeked with a week's worth of sweat and travel grime. Her hair felt tacky, and her legs throbbed from exertion and burned with chafe from the heat and saddle leather. But having Ethan constantly by her side each day, and tenderly holding her each night, had made every minute of the arduous trek worth it.

Ethan captured Lillian's gaze, his eyes alight with a fresh, new sparkle. He offered her a weary but pleased smile and tilted his head toward the next range of mountains. "That's it, Lillian, our new home."

Shielding her eyes, she turned her attention to the vast land before her. The midday sun had burned the morning mist off the Appalachian treetops and now christened the jagged summits and shaded crevices with pristine radiance. Beyond the next deep chasm, a series of blue-hued mountains rose up from the earth and circled a valley that lay hidden in the protection of their rugged inner walls.

"The mountains there are high and the valley fertile," Ethan had said. "The streams are as clear as liquid crystal, and the lake is bountiful." The Blue Haven. Lillian could see how it had earned its name. "Ethan, it's beautiful."

"I hope you still think that after you've spent two months living in a thatched-roof shelter and bathing in a cold creek."

Sweeping back a strand of hair that had worked loose from her braid, she angled her head and studied his chiseled features. His smile remained, but a trace of self-reproach haunted his jewel blue eyes. Wanting to reassure him she was exactly where she wanted to be, she reached for the hand resting on his saddle's pommel. As always, he met her halfway.

"I will, Ethan," she promised. "As long as you're there, I will."

The jesting snort of a sixteen-year-old burst the mesmerizing bubble that surrounded her and Ethan. "Cut out the lovebird talk," Billy said. "Or we'll never get there."

"Billy!" Emily scolded, while the four younger children giggled.

Face brightening with mirth, Ethan winked at Lillian, then leaned forward, his smile including the other seven people traveling with them. "Come on. We've got one more valley to cross, then we'll be home."

Shortly before sunset, they approached a narrow ravine leading into The Blue Haven. They stopped while Ethan and Jim spoke a few words of greeting to two Cherokee men standing guard outside the entrance, then rode single file through the tight passageway.

Lillian's nerves started jumping. She was about to meet her mother-in-law.

As the walls of the gully fanned away, a sparse, primitive-looking community spread out before Lillian in an area that had been partially cleared of trees. At least a dozen rectangular-shaped thatched-roof shelters spotted the rim of the valley floor. The walls of the shelters were made of heavy cloth, buckskin, canvas—whatever material the Cherokee had on hand—and were rolled up and tied to keep the heat of the day from building inside the modest, temporary homes. To the right, where the light of the western sun still heated the dale, several men, women, and adolescent children worked a field of vegetables and knee-high corn. To the left, several more men and women worked with pieces of material or animal skin.

One by one, the residents looked up. They studied the arrivals long enough to establish recognition, then laid aside the tools and ambled forward. One woman, who had been working on an animal skin, broke away from the others and dashed forward, running directly toward Ethan. *"Itana! Emeli!"* she yelled, waving her hand in excitement. *"Wili!"*

Lillian recognized Ethan's name, *Itana*, in his native tongue.

Dark-haired and fair-skinned, the Cherokee woman ran with the grace of a doe. Her radiant face brimmed with joy as she raced toward Ethan.

Jealousy clutched Lillian's throat. Who was this woman? An old girlfriend waiting for him?

"Mother," Ethan said, his low voice full of affection.

The green-eyed monster released Lillian's throat so fast, she almost fell off her saddle.

Ethan dismounted and caught the racing woman in his arms, lifting her off the ground. Emily, Billy, Jim, and the children gathered around to wait their turn to greet their beloved relative. Lillian remained on her mount, allowing the woman to greet her family without the distraction of a stranger.

Ethan's mother clung to her son like it had been three years since she'd seen him instead of three months. Lillian cast a glance at Ethan's two siblings. Emily's face was wreathed in approval and admiration. But Billy? His smile didn't exactly mirror what his gaze belied. His gray eyes held a trace of pain—and a hint of envy.

Lillian fought a fierce urge to dismount and gather the lanky young man in her arms, but she could never give him back what he must feel he'd lost by not being his mother's favorite son—the one conceived in love.

Feet still dangling above the ground, Ethan's mother drew

back, kissing his cheek, then framed his face with small, work-roughened hands. "Ethan, my son, we didn't expect you for at least two more days."

"We ran into a little trouble with the pony clubs, so we had to leave early."

A flash of panic streaked across his mother's face. "Is everyone all right?"

"Everyone is fine," Ethan assured her, "thanks to a guardian angel." Releasing his mother, he cast a quick glance Lillian's way.

Lillian disagreed with his silent insinuation. He had been the guardian angel that day, not her. All she had done was react to a critical situation. He, in turn, had chosen to come after her and rescue her from certain death, knowing his actions would result in adverse consequences for his family and their planned flight to The Blue Haven.

When his mother turned to her other family members, Ethan circled Lillian's horse to help her down. "I didn't realize you were so shy," he said as he lifted her to the ground.

"I'm not," she whispered for his ears only. "I am only nervous."

His eyes crinkled. "You have no reason to be. I'm certain you and my mother will love each other."

"I hope so." She drew in a bracing breath, and pivoted to find an aged Cherokee standing less than two feet away from her. His gray hair flowed from a center part to curve gracefully around his proud shoulders. A large feather and a small dream catcher hung from one side of his hair. A necklace of bear claws circled his neck. He studied her with dark, penetrating eyes set in a weathered, coppery face.

Lillian's mind blurred. Who was he? What should she do? What should she say?

As if he read her mind and wanted to offer support, Ethan touched the small of her back. "Lillian, this is my great-grandfather, The Pathfinder." Looking to the elder, Ethan spoke in his native tongue.

Of course, Lillian should have known his great-grandfather

would be there to greet them. She extended her right hand. "It's nice to meet you, Chief Pathfinder. Ethan's told me a lot about you."

The Pathfinder ignored her outstretched hand and used both of his own in dramatic gestures as he spoke in his native tongue. Lillian looked to Ethan for interpretation.

"He said the one I have chosen has kind eyes and a generous heart, but your spirit is strong and fighting."

The Pathfinder said a few more words while waving his expressive hands.

Again, Lillian looked to Ethan. He leveled his great-grandfather with an expression of both chagrin and affection, then turned to Lillian. "He said your strong spirit will be good for my stubborn head."

Lillian beamed at the older man. "Tell him I think he and I are going to get along just fine."

As though he understood without interpretation, a merry twinkle rose in the elder's eyes. Nodding, he moved on to greet the others.

Lillian scanned the rest of her new family to see her mother-in-law reaching for Billy. Instead of returning his mother's embrace, the buoyant youth bent down and swooped her up into the cradle of his arms, spinning her around. The gathered crowd stepped back, dodging the woman's flailing legs.

His mother threw her head back and laughed. The melodic sound of her glee danced throughout the valley.

When Billy set his mother down, she reached up and cupped his face with her hands, just as she had Ethan's. "Billy, my baby boy, I have missed you so much. The last three months have been bleak without the sound of your laughter."

Clearly, she adored her youngest child. Yet Lillian still sensed something more existed between Ethan and his mother; a special bond that reached a little beyond the norm for a mother and son, and Billy sensed it. But, then, Ethan and his mother had spent a day in hell together, and survived. They shared a nightmare the rest of the Walker family couldn't comprehend—including Lillian.

Finally, the woman finished greeting her family and, with a pleasant smile curving her lips, turned and strolled up to Lillian.

Her husband's arm around her was supportive, yet Lillian held her breath in anticipation. What would her mother-in-law think of her? How would she feel about her son marrying a white woman, especially without his mother's prior approval? Lillian supposed she was about to find out.

For a small space in time, her mother-in-law said nothing. Just stared at Lillian with dark eyes full of perception and lips curved in greeting. Her gaze seemed to slip beyond Lillian's, as though the Cherokee woman had the uncanny ability to see inside Lillian's soul, discover what her heart was made of.

Finally, the raven-haired woman tilted her head and peered up at her son. "You brought a wife," she said simply.

"Yes, Mother, I did. This is Lillian. My bride of one week." He urged Lillian forward.

She took one small, resistant step. "It's nice to meet you, Miss Walker." She was careful not to use the title of "Mistress" since Ethan had told her that his father had died before he and his mother married.

She grasped Lillian's hands. "Please, Lillian, call me Snowbird. Hopefully, you will soon feel comfortable enough to call me Mother, as my other children do."

The tension began to seep from Lillian's shoulders. "Thank you. It's an honor to be a member of such a fine family."

Hooking her arm through Lillian's, Snowbird said, "Come, you must be tired and hungry. I will fix you something to eat."

Lillian cast a bewildered glance at her husband. What was this? No interrogation? No Who-are-you? Where-did-you-come-from? What-are-your-religious-beliefs? questions?

Lillian allowed her mother-in-law to guide her toward a large, black kettle hanging by a wooden frame over an open fire. The children ran ahead. Emily, Jim, and Billy followed. Ethan fell into step beside Lillian.

As though sensing Lillian's befuddlement, Snowbird angled her head and looked at her new daughter-in-law. "What?"

"Nothing," Lillian returned a bit too quickly.

A knowing smile tipped Snowbird's lips. "Did you expect me to be a little more curious about my son's new wife?"

"I suppose," Lillian admitted.

"I am. But the questions can wait until tomorrow. Tonight, my wayward family needs food and rest. Besides"—she gave one shoulder a nonchalant shrug—"my son is a very wise man. I'm sure I will approve."

Lillian's last remnant of discomfiture melted away. Ethan was right, she decided. She was going to love her mother-in-law.

❦

After a meal of fish and mush, Snowbird passed out clean blankets to her family, then retrieved a black bear pelt from her shelter. Ethan recognized the fur blanket as the one he'd dressed and given to her three years ago for Christmas.

"Come," she said, reaching for Lillian's hand, "I'll show you where your shelter is."

"You mean, it's already built?" Lillian asked.

"Yes. We're trying to prepare for those we expect to arrive over the next few weeks. We set up Ethan's just today."

Slipping his arm around his wife's shoulder, Ethan followed his mother's lead to the last shelter on the end opposite the entrance, which pleased him. But it didn't surprise him. His mother knew how much he treasured his privacy, which was even more precious to him now.

When they stopped outside the thatched-roof shelter with buckskin walls, Snowbird held out the pelt to Ethan. "A wedding gift for you and Lillian."

"Mother, I can't take that."

"It's what I've always planned for you, since the day you gave it to me." Glancing down at the pelt, she caressed its shiny fur. "You were so proud of this. We had plenty of meat that winter."

Ethan remembered. He had been proud of the kill. It had been the first black bear he had seen in a long time, and the last one since that bountiful hunting trip. Like everything else important to his people's survival, wild game had been depleted by the intrusion.

He opened his mouth to speak, but Snowbird cut off his argument with an upheld hand. "You must take it. It's my wish. It will be my blessing."

Ethan could see his mother was sincere, and if he refused the gift, he feared he'd hurt her feelings. Reaching out, he took the pelt.

Snowbird then turned to Lillian and held out a green dress. "For you."

Lillian shook her head. "I can't—"

"Yes, you can. I have plenty."

Snowbird had three, unless she had made more since leaving Adela three months ago. The green one, Ethan remembered, was her favorite. But knowing his mother received joy in giving, and his wife really did need a second dress, he remained quiet.

Lillian hesitated an indecisive moment, then meekly reached out and accepted the dress. "Thank you."

Snowbird soon bid them good night, and as she walked away, Ethan turned to his wife. Several strands of hair had worked loose from her braid and hung like limp yarn around her sweat- and dust-streaked face. Six days of travel dirt coated her light blue dress. Exhaustion haunted the dark circles beneath her eyes.

He trapped her chin between his thumb and forefinger. "You need to rest."

"Yes, I do." She dropped her forehead to his chest. "But I'm too dirty to sleep."

He kissed the top of her head. "So am I." Raising the flap of their shelter, he tossed the pelt and blanket inside, then swept Lillian up into the cradle of his arms. "Come on, my lovely wife, I'll show you the lake."

❧

Content and rested, Ethan lay on his makeshift pelt bed the next morning, one arm folded behind his head. His wife sat close by with her back to him while she braided her white-gold hair. Even though he had been consumed by their trek northward since they'd married, he had experienced more joy during that time than he had his entire life. They had worked together, prayed together, read God's Word together, and laughed at the most trivial things.

More and more, he was learning her likes and dislikes, her little idiosyncrasies and character traits that made her delightfully unique. He'd also discovered what great fun it was to tease her, and exactly what kind of prankishness would ruffle those pretty, blond feathers of hers.

"Wife," he said, forcing a stern note to his voice, "go get my breakfast and bring it to me."

She stopped in the middle of tying a string around the end of her braid and slowly turned her head, leveling him with a scathing glare. "What did you say?"

He struggled to hold a straight face. He'd learned, rather quickly, she didn't take orders well. Ask her to do something or make a polite request, and she'd do anything. But never, ever order her to do something. She demanded as much respect as she gave, which was a lot. And that was only one of the things he found so appealing about her.

"I said, 'Go get my breakfast and bring it to me,'" he repeated. "I wish to eat in bed this morning."

"And I wish to be the next president."

Ethan had no doubt she'd make a great one, if ever given the opportunity. He raised what he hoped looked like a chiding brow. "'Wives, submit yourselves unto your own husbands.' Isn't that what we read last night?"

"We also read 'Husbands, love your wives, even as Christ also loved the church, and gave himself for it.'"

"Oh, but this husband does."

"Good," she quipped, and turned her attention back to securing her braid.

"Does this mean you're not going to submit?"

She glanced back over her shoulder, a daring spark shimmering in her eyes. "What if it does?" she responded, her voice now low and brimming with an unspoken challenge.

Ethan knew she wasn't looking for an argument. She was vying for another kind of attention, and he was happy to oblige.

Their gazes locked in an intense stare down, and the energy of a dozen lightning bolts charged the air between them. Propping up on one arm, Ethan narrowed his eyes. "Then, I suppose I'll have to. . ." In one swift move, he reached for her. "*Kiss* you into submission."

She released a squeal brimming with laughter and half-heartedly attempted to dodge his hand. But the instant his fingers circled her wrist, she fell willingly into his arms.

Their mouths merged with rehearsed ease. Ethan soon forgot about the emptiness in his stomach. But the taste of his wife's lips, the smell of her skin, and the softness in her touch stirred a deeper hunger only she could satisfy.

When she drew back, she grinned like a lioness that had just devoured her prey. "Remind me not to submit more often."

"Every chance I get." He circled the back of her neck with his hand and pulled her to him once again.

Breakfast could wait.

❧

Some time later, Lillian and Ethan sat down on a blanket outside Snowbird's shelter. They were the last to join the Walker family for breakfast.

"It's about time," Emily said, offering Ethan a tin plate of food along with a knowing grin. "I thought you two were going to sleep all day."

Ethan winked at Lillian as he reached for his food. "We were tempted to."

Ducking her head to hide her warming cheeks, Lillian accepted her own plate of biscuits and fried meat. Her husband loved to tease her, sometimes relentlessly. In the short time they'd been married, he'd figured out exactly what would make her blush or what would raise her hackles.

But, at other times, like when she was frustrated with learning something new, or she was tired and cranky, his gentle patience and tender touch soothed her in a way nothing else could. He seemed to know just what she needed and when she needed it.

Taking her first bite of meat, she filtered a dreamy sigh. She never imagined being in love would be so beautiful. Already, it seemed, every breath she took depended on the one Ethan had just taken.

She felt guilty about leaving the children in Adela without a teacher so suddenly. And grief plagued her because she had to leave her father without telling him where she was going and why she'd left so suddenly. But, other than that, she didn't have a single regret she was there with Ethan, her husband, her lifeline.

Snowbird, who sat on Lillian's other side, set down her plate and turned to Lillian. "Tell me a little about yourself," she said. "How did my son find you? Where did you come from?"

"Oh, yes!" Snowbird's questions brought to mind something Ethan had told Lillian during their journey to The Blue Haven, and she couldn't wait to tell her mother-in-law about it. "Snowbird, Ethan told me you went to the missionary school at Spring Place."

Snowbird's eyelashes fluttered, and the pleasantness in her expression dimmed. "I did."

Lillian squeezed Snowbird's hand. Maybe what she had to share would banish that sad look from her mother-in-law's face. "My grandparents were missionary teachers at Spring Place, and my father spent most of his youth there. Ethan and I compared dates, and you and my father were both there at the same time. Perhaps you remember him. His name is—"

"Marcus," Snowbird said in a throaty whisper.

"That's right. Marcus Gunter is my father."

The cup slipped from Snowbird's grasp, spilling tea in her lap. She jerked her hand away like Lillian's touch had suddenly burned her. "*No*. He can't be."

Lillian blinked in befuddlement. "Yes, he is." Her mind told her she should do something, but the look of shock and horror on her mother-in-law's face paralyzed her ability to react.

Snowbird started trembling.

"Mother?" Ethan said.

"Snowbird?" Jim followed. "What's wrong?"

Setting aside his plate, Ethan shuffled around Lillian and kneeled in front of his mother, grasping her upper arms. The others gathered around, except for Lillian. Snowbird's frozen glare still had Lillian pinned down.

"Mother." Ethan gave the stunned woman a firm shake. "Tell me what's wrong."

Ethan's efforts seemed to penetrate his mother's stunned mind. Slowly, she turned her head to stare at her son, her shock turning into a tortuous pain. Tears sprang into her eyes. With quivering hands, she bracketed his face. "Ethan, *Itana*, my son, you have no idea what you have done."

thirteen

Ethan stood on The Blue Haven's lakeshore, out of sight and hearing distance from everyone else in the valley, except his mother. She stood at the water's edge with her back to him, her arms wrapped tightly around her waist. From her disturbing reaction a while ago, he knew she had something of great significance to tell him, but he couldn't fathom what it was.

He waited to see if she would initiate the conversation. When she didn't, he said, "Talk to me, Mother."

She drew in a deep, shuddery breath, releasing it in a long, withering sigh. "You and Lillian figured right; Marcus and I were at Spring Place together. She allowed at least five seconds to crawl by. "For a long time, we were just friends. But somewhere along the way, that friendship turned into love."

Surprise shot through Ethan. "You mean, you were in love with Lillian's father?"

"Yes. I was sixteen, and he was eighteen when he asked me to marry him."

Ethan couldn't believe what he was hearing. His mother. . . and Lillian's father. . .engaged? His brow dipped in thought. Obviously, the engagement hadn't worked out, because his mother had never been married. "What happened?"

"His father didn't approve."

"Because you are Cherokee?" Ethan guessed.

"Because I am Cherokee. Because we were so young, so naïve about how we would be treated by bigots. . .and about the future of our people. At least that's what Marcus's father told him," she added, her voice laced with bitterness.

Ethan's mother was actually half-blood—as much white as she was Cherokee. Apparently that hadn't mattered to Marcus's father. But what about Marcus?

"Marcus believed the only way we could be together was to

145

prove to his father that he was prepared to support a wife and family," she said, as though reading his mind. "So he joined the United States Army in 1811. He planned to come home on his first leave, find us a place to live, and marry me. The night before he left, we slipped out to our secret meeting place, near the herb garden." Again, she paused. "We only meant to say good-bye. . . ." She didn't explain further. She didn't have to.

"What are you saying, Mother? That you and Marcus Gunter had an affair?"

"What I'm saying, Ethan, is that Marcus Gunter is your father."

"My father is dead," he returned automatically, as he had done all of his life.

She turned and faced him, and the look of penitent sorrow on her teary face twisted Ethan's gut. "No, Ethan, he isn't," she said, her arms still clinging to her waist.

Numbed by shock, he stared at her in stunned silence. This had to be a dream, a bad dream from which he'd soon awaken. That's why he couldn't feel anything, couldn't think beyond the minute the sun would rise and banish this ludicrous vision from his head.

Snowbird started to tremble. "Lillian. . .is your half sister."

The words hung between them for a few frozen seconds. Then, like blood dripping from a severed vein, the feeling trickled back into Ethan's body. His hands grew heavy, like dead limbs dangling from a tree. The onerous sensation moved up his arms, filled his chest, pushed up his throat. Finally, it rolled off his tongue in one husky word of denial. *"No."*

Tears dripped off Snowbird's chin. "Yes, Ethan, I'm afraid she is." She shook her head in remorse. "I am sorry. I am so, so sorry."

His legs almost buckled. Bewilderment attacked his mind. *No, no, no!* rolled over and over in his mind. Disappointment in the woman standing in front of him clawed at his chest. "Why, Mother? *If* Marcus Gunter is my father, why have you told me all these years he was dead?"

"For a long time, I thought he was. His father told me Marcus was killed in a training exercise six weeks after he left Spring Place. I only found out Marcus was alive after Emma and Frederick moved to our village, and she mentioned that her younger brother, Marcus Gunter, was an army officer."

Like the shifting wind, Ethan's bewilderment crystallized into anger. "Ten years? You've known my father was alive for ten years, and you never told me?"

"He had a wife, a daughter, and a prosperous life. I had you, Emily, and Billy, and we were struggling to keep the gristmill my father had left us running. Marcus had chosen to marry someone else. I feared that he would reject you and your sister. . .as he had rejected me."

"Who else knows, Mother? Who else has made a fool of me, pretending to be my friend while they lied to me about my father? Frederick and Emma? Jim?"

"No, Ethan. No one. Emma and Fredrick still lived in Virginia then, so I had no way of knowing she was Macus's sister until after she moved to Adela. And I never told anyone who your father was. After I was told Marcus was dead, I left the missionary school and never returned. When I learned I was with child, I was afraid that Marcus's father would take my only link to Marcus away from me and give you to his older daughter to raise as her own. I couldn't bear thinking that my child would be raised in their prejudiced world. And when I found out that Marcus was alive I feared that you would choose him over me if I told you the truth. Marcus could offer you so much more."

For the first time in his life, Ethan felt like his mother had slapped him. "Well, thank you, Mother," he sneered. "It's nice to know you had so much confidence in me."

She held out her palms in a beseeching gesture. "You were *sixteen* years old, Ethan. A young man who'd had to grow up too fast. You wanted things I couldn't give you. Things Marcus could." She swung her head from side to side. "I wasn't willing to take that risk."

"So you lived a lie for the last ten years to suit your own

selfish needs." Ethan had never talked to his mother with such rancor, but he couldn't help it. His and Lillian's life together had just been destroyed, all because of his mother's dishonesty.

"I did what I thought was best at the time."

Her eyes pleaded for understanding, but Ethan didn't understand. He never would. She had just snuffed out the one bright light in his life. "What about me, Mother?" He slammed his fist against his chest. "What about Lillian? What do you think this is going to do to her?"

Snowbird pursed her lips. "I don't know."

Ethan knew—exactly. It was going to squeeze the life from her—just like it was him.

He struggled to breathe. How could this be? If Lillian was his sister, why did he love her as a husband loves a wife? Why had he felt so certain God sanctioned their marriage? In desperation, he grasped for one last thread. "Mother, are you absolutely certain Marcus Gunter is my father?"

She didn't look offended, only repentant. "In my lifetime, I have been with only one man willingly."

Marcus Gunter. Lillian's father. Ethan's father.

An acute sense of loss swept through Ethan, leaving him weak and jerking. What was he going to do? He raked a shaky hand through his hair. He needed to clear his head so he could think. . .and pray. "I need to be alone for a while."

She ducked her head and turned to go.

"Mother?" When she looked back, he said, "Don't say anything to Lillian about this."

Snowbird inclined her head.

"Tell her I will be home before dark."

Again, Snowbird nodded, then held his gaze for another agonizing moment. "I truly am sorry, Ethan," she said, barely above a whisper.

But Ethan looked away. His mother's apology, like the truth, had come just a little too late.

He waited until she was gone, then cupped one hand over his face. What was he going to do? What *should* he do? What was right? For Lillian? For him? For the both of them? She was his wife, the love of his life. But she was also his sister, and their love was forbidden. A dizzying wave of hopelessness washed through him, leaving behind a deep, gaping wound. His legs buckled, and he fell to his knees. He wanted to die.

Like a hurtling arrow, a harrowing idea shot through his mind. Just as quickly, he shoved it away. He couldn't take his own life. That would be wrong, go against everything he now believed in. And he had to think about Lillian.

A searing pain ripped through him. Lillian, who had brought joy into his desolate life, taught him how to laugh again, had shown him the meaning of unconditional love. Lillian, who had given up everything. . .for him.

A wrenching sob tore from his throat and quaked across his shoulders. Dear God, how was he going to tell her this? What was it going to do to her? Hot tears rolled down his cheeks. He began to rock. *Why, God, why?*

Ethan didn't sense his Heavenly Father's presence. The grief was too great, the pain too overwhelming. He bowed his forehead to the ground and breathed in deep, burning breaths. His nostrils and mouth filled with the smell and taste of the dry, insipid soil. He pounded the stony earth with his fist, and rocked his head from side to side. *Please, God, please don't turn away from me now. I know my faith is weak, and my mind filled with doubt, but I can't do this alone. I need You.*

He stretched out prostrate on the ground, laid his head on his folded arms, and continued to cry out in desperation.

❧

A shake of his shoulder aroused Ethan. "Ethan, are you all right?"

Ethan raised his heavy head, blinking through the blinding brightness of the day to look at Jim, who knelt beside him. "What is it?"

"You've been gone a long time. We were concerned."

He rolled over to his back and lay there a moment with his forearm across his sun-dazzled eyes. How could he have fallen asleep with what he and Lillian were facing? He forced a swallow past the stickiness in his parched throat. "Did Mother tell you?" he asked.

"Yes."

Ethan lunged up to a sitting position, took the canteen Jim held out to him, and drank. After wiping his gritty mouth with his shirtsleeve, he handed the water vessel back to Jim. Then, propping his elbows on his bent knees, he funneled his fingers through his hair and held his forehead in his palms. "What am I going to do, Jim?"

"I honestly don't know, Ethan. I wish I did."

A tremendous weight pressed down upon Ethan's chest, like mighty rocks had fallen from the mountaintop and buried him. "The love I feel for Lillian is so different than what I feel for Emily."

"I know." A silence heavy with thought passed. "I've thought about you ever since Snowbird told me this morning, and I've asked myself a hundred times what I would do. The only thing that comes back to me is that you said your marriage vows to Lillian before you knew she was your sister."

Ethan closed his eyes, wishing he could as easily close off the horrible nightmare haunting him. "I've thought about that. But if we were to continue living together as husband and wife, knowing she's my sister will be between us every time I touch her." Memories from the week before rushed into his mind. Memories he had, just that morning, reflected on with a sense of reverence and beauty. A sick feeling rose from the pit of his stomach. He tried to swallow it, and couldn't. His mother's lie had even soiled what he and Lillian had already shared.

Jim gently grasped Ethan's wrist, pulled down his arm, and laid a worn, black Bible in his hand. "I don't have the answer, Ethan. But somewhere among these pages, there is one. I've marked a few places. It may not make things easier in the days ahead, but maybe it'll show you what to do." He placed a firm hand on Ethan's shoulder. "I'll be praying for you. Let me know if there's anything I can do." With that, Jim rose and walked away.

Ethan stared at the book for a long time. Yes, he'd probably find an answer there, but did he want to know what it was? Shoulders slumping in defeat, he scrubbed a weary hand down his face. What other choice did he have?

Opening the Bible in his lap, he began reading, starting with the first place Jim had marked. By the time he finished, he knew what he had to do, but he didn't know *how* he was going to do it. So he bowed his head and prayed for strength.

&

Shortly before sunset, Ethan rose and headed back to the camp. He had promised Lillian he would be home before dark, and he would keep his word to her. He had prayed and meditated all afternoon, but he still didn't know how he was going to find the strength to tell her they shared the same father.

The second he stepped into the camp, he saw her, sitting alone outside their shelter, reading a book. As though sensing his approach, she looked up. Laying the book aside, she vaulted up and ran to him, throwing herself in his arms.

A landslide of tumultuous emotions tumbled through him, making his body tremble. Or was it hers? He wrapped his arms around her slight frame and realized it was both. She knew something was wrong. Something ominous and dreadful. Closing his eyes, he cupped the back of her head with one hand and buried his face in her hair. *Oh, God, help me tell her. Then, when I do, help her.*

His arms tightened around her, as hers did around him. A deep and unyielding ache threatened to smother him. How were they ever going to get through this?

After a time—Ethan wasn't sure how long—their trembling ceased. Simultaneously, they drew back to meet each other's gaze. He brushed the hair away from her face, and there in her questioning eyes, he found his strength. For her, he could be strong. For her, he could do anything. Even let her go—if that's what she wanted. With great effort, he breathed past the tightness restricting his lungs.

Hand in hand, they made the trek to their shelter. Before ducking inside, Lillian picked up her Bible, the book she had apparently been reading when he appeared. They sat down facing each other, their legs crisscrossed. Lillian didn't say or ask anything. Just waited.

Leaning forward, Ethan propped his elbows on his knees and grasped her slim, pale hands. Somehow, by the grace of God, he repeated everything his mother had told him. While he spoke, every emotion he'd experienced one hundred times over that day—shock, denial, hurt—marred Lillian's lovely features. He finished with the words he dreaded most: "Lillian, you are my half sister."

Her eyelids fluttered, once. She stared at him a dazed moment, then pulled her hands from his and grasped the front of his shirt. "No, Ethan, this cannot be. You are my husband. I am your wife."

He cupped her fisted hands with his palms. His eyes burned, blurring her desperate face. "Yes, Lillian. You are my wife. But you are also my sister."

"No!" She shook her head in denial. "No, no, no!" Releasing his shirt, she pounded his chest with each fiery word.

Understanding her reaction, Ethan sat like a stone statue, taking the blows. She wasn't striking out at him. She was striking out at Fate and the lie that had tainted their love.

He knew how she felt.

When her arms fell limp, he pulled her onto his lap. She collapsed against his chest, a heartrending sob tearing through her body. As he wrapped his arms around her quaking body, a smoldering spark of anger flared inside him. His mother had done this to Lillian. His own mother. How could he ever forgive her?

By the time Lillian's tears were spent, night had long fallen. She pushed away from him and fumbled around in the dark until she found and lit a candle. Then, sitting with her profile facing him, she drew up her legs beneath her skirt and hugged her knees to her chest.

He wanted so much to brush the hair away from her face, kiss the pain out of her wounded, green eyes, but right now, he was afraid to touch her. They were both too vulnerable.

She released a shuddery sigh. "What are we going to do, Ethan?" she asked, her voice small and forlorn.

He sucked in a deep, bracing breath. "Lillian, I will always hold our vows sacred. Right here"—he pressed his fist over his heart—"you are my wife, and nothing will ever change that. But, by blood, you are my sister." He swallowed, painfully. "We can no longer share a marriage bed. It is forbidden in God's Word. If you stay, that must change, but that is the only thing. However, if you decide to go back to Virginia, I won't try to stop you. Just know that whatever you decide, I will always remain faithful to you. There will never be another. . .there never could be."

Her chin quivered, and her eyes watered. "For me either."

He forced a small smile that felt as sad as their grief. "Take some time to think about it. Either way, I'll understand. I only want what's best for you."

He reached up and caressed her cheek. As always, the satiny softness of her skin amazed him. He was going to miss touching her so much. His bleeding heart lurched, and he almost came undone. He dropped his hand, and a desolate chill rattled through him. He needed to get out of there, before he did something he'd hate himself for tomorrow.

"I will sleep outside our shelter tonight. Tomorrow, I will set up another next to this one. I will never be so far away that I can't hear your call if you need me."

She nodded, and he lunged for the buckskin flap. Before he could dart outside, she grabbed his arm, stopping him. In his crouched position, he twisted his head around and looked at her.

"Stay with me tonight, Ethan."

A spasm of desire shot through him. He closed his eyes in agony. "Lillian—"

"Not in that way. I only want you to hold me. Just let me feel your arms around me one more time. . .please?"

Her soft plea and beseeching green eyes shredded Ethan's weak cord of resistance. If holding her one last time would help get her through this night, then that's what he would do, and, somehow, he'd survive it without dishonoring her.

He lay down atop the blanket covering the fur pelt. She blew out the candle and crawled beneath the blanket, curling into his side. Wrapping his arms around her, he stared up into a darkness he wished would never end. Because, after tonight, he could never hold her like this again.

"Ethan?"

"Yes."

"I'll stay."

Mixed emotions rolled through him. His eyes slid shut. That's exactly what he'd hope for, and exactly what he'd feared. How could he survive seeing her every day and not touching her? Would it be as hard as not seeing her at all? "Are you sure that's what you want?"

"Yes. If I can't be with you like this, then I will settle for just being near you." Three torturous seconds passed. "That will be enough."

Ethan could only hope so—for both their sakes.

Dampness seeped into his shirt, and he knew she was crying again. But this time her tears were silent.

So were his.

fourteen

Lillian lay curled on her side, listening to the people stir outside her shelter. She should be up, helping cook breakfast. But today she simply couldn't find the strength.

Two weeks ago, Ethan had said the only thing that would change would be their living arrangements, but he had been wrong. So wrong. She had not only lost the feel of her husband's strong arms around her, she had lost her joy, her hope, her desire to get up and face each new day. And so had he. She saw it in the hollowness of his eyes every time she looked at him, and the slump of his shoulders. He didn't walk as straight and tall as he once did.

Oh, he'd tried to put on a good face—for her sake. But he couldn't hide the deep pain ripping him apart, not from her. Loving each other from afar was tearing them both down. She didn't know how much more either of them could endure.

She rolled to her back, wincing when her stomach churned. Her misery was even beginning to affect her health. For the last two mornings, she had awakened feeling ill. She laid her forearm across her eyes and waited for the queasiness to pass. Maybe she should go back to Virginia when the removal was over. Perhaps if she did, Ethan could eventually get on with his life. She never would. But there was no reason he should continue to suffer. And if she stayed, he surely would.

"Lillian, may I come in?"

Oh, no. Ethan. He'd probably brought her breakfast—again. She shuddered at the thought of eating, and tried to swallow the fullness in her throat. That was another reason she needed to leave. He worried about her constantly, the same way she did him. "Give me just a minute."

155

She sat up, grabbing her stomach when it lurched again. If this continued, she would have to talk to Emily about a remedy.

When the nausea passed, she combed her fingers through her tousled hair. She hadn't even braided it the last two nights and would probably never brush out the tangles. Not that she really cared. Maybe she'd just cut off the bothersome mess, so she'd have one less aggravation to worry about.

She released a wearisome sigh. No time to contemplate what to do with her waist-length mane now. Ethan wasn't a very patient man lately.

She tied her hair back with a leather strap, then pinched her cheeks, hoping to bring some color to her face. Then, clasping her hands in her lap, she drew back her shoulders. "All right, you may come in now."

He pulled back the flap and laid it over the top of the shelter, leaving the "door" open. *Of course,* she thought with bitter sarcasm, *we wouldn't want to give the neighbors a reason to talk.*

Guilt pricked her conscience even as the thoughts evolved. Ethan didn't deserve having her ire directed at him. It wasn't his fault their lives were in such a wretched state of limbo. Deep down, she knew it was no one's fault. Yet she harbored a growing anger she couldn't control. If she didn't find a way to release it soon, she was going to explode.

"Good morning," Ethan said, forcing a smile that didn't reach his eyes. He ducked inside, holding out a plate. "I brought you some breakfast."

When Lillian looked at the fried meat, biscuit, and sawmill gravy, her stomach rebelled. Clamping her hand over her mouth, she lunged outside.

❧

Elbows on bent knees, forehead in his palms, Ethan waited outside the shelter while Emily examined Lillian. He couldn't banish the picture of her violent retching, or the way she had collapsed in his arms when her stomach finally emptied.

Shame wrapped its ugly hands around him. He should have followed his first instincts and sent her back to Adela, but he hadn't. He'd married her and brought her here, to this destitute valley, where she'd caught some dreadful disease. A heavy ache squeezed his chest. He could only pray now that God would give him another chance to get her to Virginia, where she belonged.

He noticed a slight disturbance in the air and raised his head to find Emily, medicine basket in hand, coming out of the shelter. His weary body tensed. "How is she?"

Patting his arm, his twin sister offered him a complacent smile. "I'll let her tell you."

Without hesitation, Ethan crawled into the shelter, but stopped short as the flap fell behind him. To his surprise, Lillian was sitting up, braiding her hair. How could this be? A few minutes ago, she'd been too weak to open her eyes.

She met his gaze with a warm smile. Alarm clashed with relief. She hadn't smiled in two weeks. Could she be delirious?

After securing her braid, she reached out to him. He shuffled forward and sat down facing her, grasping her outstretched hands in his. Caressing her knuckles with his thumbs, he searched her face. Dark circles still ringed her eyes, but her skin wasn't as ashen as it had been a while ago. "How do you feel?"

"Still a little weak, but the queasiness is gone."

"Does Emily know what made you so sick?"

A faint sparkle rose in her eyes. "Yes. We're going to have a baby."

Surprise stilled the thumbs caressing her hands. "A baby?"

She nodded.

Ethan had, over the last fourteen days, considered the possibility of Lillian being with child. But he hadn't expected symptoms so soon—or so violent—as Lillian's. Even while mourning her husband's death, Emily had carried the twins without a single episode of morning sickness. "But we've only been married three weeks. Isn't it too early to tell?"

Remorse dulled the brightness in Lillian's eyes. She lowered her gaze. "Emily said I'm already getting sick because my body has been deprived of food and rest."

Guilt merged with Ethan's surprise. He tipped her chin. "I should have taken better care of you."

"I should have taken better care of myself," she said, her tone laced with reproach. Then the sparkle returned to her eyes. "A baby, Ethan. Isn't that amazing?"

He studied her face, and saw there a peace he had feared he'd never see again. "You're happy about this," he concluded.

He wasn't sure yet how he felt about the pregnancy. What were the chances of him and Lillian having a normal, healthy baby?

Lillian glanced away for a ponderous moment. "Ethan, for the last two weeks, I've had this ugly anger growing inside me. I blamed God for leading us to each other only to have us discover we are brother and sister."

Ethan knew the feeling. He was still angry with God. . .and his mother.

Looking back at him, she shook her head. "It's not God's fault, Ethan, or anyone else's. It's simply a cruel stroke of fate —one I'm finding very hard to accept." She ducked her head. "I've wanted to die since you told me. I even asked God a couple of times to take my life." She raised her lashes, revealing green eyes glistening with moisture. "Instead, He gave me a reason to live. In that reason, He reminded me of the most beautiful week of my life." She reached up and touched his cheek. "That's a memory that will live in my heart forever." Her misty gaze caressed his face. "I have no regrets, Ethan."

Something happened inside him, something that cracked the ice that had formed around his heart, and he was reminded of something his twin sister had told him. "Emily said something like that to me the day you and I married. She said she would go through the grief of losing her husband all over again, just to have one more day with him."

Lillian's chin quivered. "As I would with you."

And Ethan would with Lillian. He knew that with a certainty he couldn't explain. But he still couldn't ignore the disturbing possibility plaguing his mind. He framed Lillian's face with his hands. "Lillian, sometimes, when close relatives have a child—"

"I know. Emily told me. But I also know God doesn't make mistakes. For some reason, He brought us together and gave us this child. No matter what, our baby will know he or she is loved and wanted, a precious gift God has sent to help us carry the burden we've been given to bear."

In the dark cavern that had consumed Ethan's soul, a tiny ray of hope winked. What Lillian said was true. In the midst of their grievous storm, God had sent them a precious gift, a symbol of their love. There would still be heartache, but God would sustain them. Perhaps, someday, even restore their joy.

He looked deep into his wife's eyes and again saw that overflowing well of promise and devotion he had missed so much, a silent message telling him that her heart would always be joined with his. The corners of his mouth tipped of their own volition. Whatever made him think he could send her away? Even if he wanted to, even if he tried, she would never go. They were bound together by a power stronger than the human spirit.

Lillian sweetened the air with a sad sigh of acceptance. "If all I can do is sit beside you and watch our child grow, Ethan, then I'll gladly take it and consider myself a woman most blessed."

In Lillian's words, Ethan found a new thread of strength and grabbed onto it. He pressed his forehead to hers. "We'll make it, Lillian. Somehow, someway, we'll get through this."

"I know we will."

He drew in a deep, replenishing breath. Her balmy scent wrapped around his senses, kindling a deeper need. Quickly tempering his desire, he pulled away, and a yawning sense of emptiness swept through him.

Yes, with God's help, they would get through this. But it sure wasn't going to be easy.

⠶

Two days later, Lillian sat in the shade of an oak tree, sewing the seams of a shirt she was making for Ethan—the outcome of which would be interesting. She had never sewn anything in her life, and now she knew why. She hated it.

Snowbird, who kneeled just a few feet away grinding dried corn with a smooth, round stone, paused in her task to inspect Lillian's progress. "When you get that sleeve stitched up, I'll show you how to attach the cuffs."

"That sounds like fun," Lillian responded dryly.

A soft chuckle escaped Snowbird's throat, and Lillian had to smile. She was so glad Ethan had made peace with his mother—for both their sakes. Snowbird still wore the haunted look of guilt. Like Ethan and Lillian, Snowbird had a grievous burden to carry. She would always have to live with what her secret had done to her son and daughter-in-law. But at least the older woman's tears fell less often now. Hopefully, she would someday find her way back to God. Only then would she know true peace.

Pulling another stitch, Lillian filtered a wistful sigh. *Peace.* Slowly but surely, hers was returning. She lifted her gaze to her husband, who stood in the center of the camp with Chief Pathfinder and several other men, discussing where they would build the new council house. They still didn't know if the government was going to allow them to stay on the land, but Ethan had persuaded his people not to wait in limbo. After all, no one knew better than he that life went on in spite of devastating circumstances.

A flutter rose beneath her ribs. She dropped her busy hands to her lap and pursed her lips. Her heart still tripped every time she looked at him. At night, her body ached for the comfort of his strong arms, the tender touch of his loving hands. But with God's help, she was bearing the loneliness. Whenever desolation threatened to smother her, she would turn to Him and always find His grace sufficient to bridge the gap of each aching need.

One of the men standing with Ethan pointed toward the valley entrance. The others turned to see what had captured his attention. Lillian also followed the direction of his pointing finger to find two men on horses entering the dale.

Fleeing Cherokees trickling into The Blue Haven had almost become a daily occurrence. Still, everyone stopped whatever they were doing to greet each new arrival. Lillian laid aside her sewing and rose to join her husband and his family in welcoming the refugees.

After only a few steps, she realized she knew the first rider. Uncle Frederick's black hat atop his head and black suspenders striping his white shirt were unmistakable. What was he doing here? He wasn't scheduled to arrive until the removal ended.

Shielding her eyes, she shifted her gaze to the second rider and found something profoundly familiar about him. His light brown hair glinted gold in the sun. Although dressed like a civilian, he held his back and shoulders erect, like a disciplined soldier. And his chestnut mount looked exactly like. . . .

Her steps faltered in surprise, then delight raced down her body and she set out in a run, waving her arm over her head. "Papa! Papa!"

Her father dismounted before reining in his horse and ran to meet her, wrapping her in a crushing hug. "Lillian," he said, his voice flooded with relief. "Thank God, you're all right. I've been out of my mind with worry."

Guilt stabbed at Lillian's conscience. She drew back and looked up into her father's weary face. "I'm sorry, Papa. I couldn't let you know what happened. Too much was at risk."

"You could have at least sent word you were all right."

No, she couldn't. He would have gone through Frederick and anyone else in order to find her.

Something clicked in her mind. Her father wasn't supposed to discover her whereabouts until the removal was over, and the Cherokee were no longer in danger of being forced west. Why was he here now, in the first days of the roundup? A sudden panic seized her. "How did you find out where I was? Did Uncle Frederick tell you?"

"Yes, after he received a letter from Snowbird explaining everything."

Lillian blinked. "Everything?"

"Everything."

Uneasiness slipped beneath her skin. "Then you know I'm married. . . ." The words "to my brother" lodged in her throat.

"Yes." His gaze shifted to the space over her right shoulder. "And this must be your husband."

She turned to find Ethan standing behind her. She stepped to the side and studied the two most important men in her life. Father and son stood face-to-face, almost equal in stance, parallel in determination, eyes the same shade of blue. Her hand fluttered aimlessly to her chest. She never realized, until that moment, how much the two were alike.

She glanced from one face to the other, wishing she could read their grim expressions, know what each was thinking. Who would be the first to speak? Who would make the first move? Pressing her lips into a thin line, she held her breath. . . and waited.

&

Ethan stood facing Marcus Gunter, the man who, by blood, was his father. But would he prove to be a true parent? How much would he understand? How much would he accept—or reject—of Ethan and his complex relationship with Lillian?

Ethan held his emotions in check. He had seen too much tragedy, witnessed too much pain recently to lend a piece of himself to a man he did not know—even if that man was his father.

Ethan waited for Marcus to make the first move. Finally, the older man inclined his head. "Ethan."

Ethan returned the gesture of greeting, but said nothing.

"I need to talk to you and Lillian. Can you take us to a private place?"

Again, Ethan nodded.

Marcus scanned the crowd until his gaze settled on someone. Ethan knew without looking it was his mother. An expression of reminiscent longing softened Marcus's somber features, and a heavy sadness stole over Ethan. Almost thirty years ago, one man's prejudice had robbed his mother and Marcus of a happy life together. And that same prejudice had reached down to another generation and touched Ethan and Lillian's life in much the same way.

An overwhelming sense of protection filled Ethan with new determination. The pain stopped here, he decided. He would not allow the bigotry to be passed down to his child. If that was the only good thing to come out of his and Lillian's intricate bond, then maybe he could one day see a purpose in their suffering.

Finally, Marcus swallowed, like a thirsty man craving water he could see but not reach. Then he turned his attention back to Ethan and tipped his head, indicating he was ready to follow.

❧

A dozen questions swirled in Lillian's mind as she walked with her father and Ethan to the lake's shore. What did her father have in mind? Was he going to insist she leave The Blue Haven—and Ethan? Would Ethan challenge Marcus, his own father, whom he'd never met before today? She sucked up a deep, calming breath. The last thing she wanted was her father and husband-brother fighting over her.

Once at the lake, Ethan slipped a protective arm around Lillian and turned to face Marcus with eyes full of unyielding determination. "Before you begin, I want you to know neither Lillian nor I knew we were related when we married. Since we found out, we've changed our living arrangements. But in our eyes, and in the eyes of God, we feel we did nothing wrong that first week we were married."

Marcus's grim features softened. "Ethan, you and Lillian have done nothing wrong, anyway."

Lillian's brow furrowed in confusion. Her father's response made no sense to her at all.

Ethan gave Marcus a wary look. "What do you mean?"

"I mean. . ." Marcus shifted his gaze to Lillian, his eyes dulling with something akin to regret. "Lillian, since the day you were born, you have been the center of my life, my daughter in every way. . .except by blood."

Lillian felt Ethan's body tense; his grasp tightened on her waist. But she couldn't react. What was her father trying to tell her?

"Lillian," Marcus continued, "your real father was a man named Neal Farrell. I met him after I joined the military. We belonged to the same regiment. We fought side by side during the War of 1812. When the war ended, we were stationed near Wilmington."

Stunned, Lillian could only stare at her father. Was what he was saying true? Was it possible she really wasn't Ethan's sister?

"Neal met your mother at a ball celebrating the end of the war," Marcus went on. "It was the proverbial 'love at first sight.' But he was the son of poor Irish immigrants, and her father didn't approve of their relationship."

A quick flash of rancor shot through Lillian. Another young couple's love shattered by the ugly hands of prejudice. Would the vicious cycle ever end? "Go on," she urged her father.

"They were determined to marry, with or without your grandfather's approval. Neal began saving money to buy his own place. In the meantime, he and Sarah continued seeing each other in secret. They would meet at the cabin at the back of the plantation property."

Lillian knew the building he spoke of. A run-down, neglected cabin she had seen from a distance. Her mother had always forbidden Lillian to go there. Now, she knew why—because of the bittersweet memories the forsaken cottage held.

"One day, when Neal and Sarah were supposed to meet, he didn't show up. Naturally concerned, she went looking for him. She found him about a mile away. Apparently, something had spooked his horse, and it had thrown him. His neck was broken. . .he was dead."

Struggling between guilt and ecstasy, Lillian slipped her arm around Ethan and grasped the side of his homespun shirt for support. She should feel something like grief, sadness, or sorrow over the premature death of Neal Farrell, the father she never knew. But for the moment, all she felt was mounting joy and blessed relief.

"I thought Sarah was going to die from grief," Marcus added. "I tried to comfort her, tried to be a friend. But there's little comfort to be found in the wake of losing someone you love so much."

Lillian knew her father spoke from experience, but who was he referring to? Her mother. . .or Snowbird. . .or both?

"You see, when I first enlisted in the army I had grandiose plans to come back to Spring Place during my first leave and marry Snowbird. My father didn't approve of our relationship, said we were too young, too naïve. But I was determined to prove him wrong." Marcus wore the look of a betrayed man. "My father wrote to me and told me Snowbird had died of a fever. I never would have thought him capable of lying to me."

Neither would Lillian. She had always thought her grandfather an honest and honorable man.

Marcus shook his head and sighed before continuing. "A

few weeks after Neal died, Sarah came to me and told me she was with child, and asked me what she should do."

"So you married her," Lillian concluded, "and raised me as your own."

Marcus tipped his head in confirmation.

The sweet waters filling Lillian's joy cup bubbled over, and she could no longer hold back her elation. Tears blurred her vision. A trembling hand fluttered to her pounding chest.

"I'm sorry I never told you about your real father, Lillian. I hope you can someday forgive me."

Dropping her arm from around Ethan, she stepped forward and framed her father's face with her hands. "Forgive you for what? Loving me? Raising me as your own daughter?" She shook her head in adoration for the man in front of her. "Oh, Papa, I'm sorry Neal Farrell died at what should have been the happiest time in his life, and that I never had a chance to know him. But I'm not sorry that God sent you into my life to love and take care of me as only a loving father would. *You* are my father in every sense of the word. And today you have given me the most precious gift in the world; you have given me back my husband." Feeling whole, feeling cherished, feeling blessed, Lillian wrapped her arms around her father's neck.

❧

Ethan didn't realize he was crying until he tasted the salt in his tears. So much elation filled his chest, he thought surely it would burst. He pursed his quivering lips. Was it possible to die from joy? He hoped not; he had too much to live for.

When Lillian released Marcus, the older man turned to Ethan. "What does a man say to the son who's just married his daughter?"

A bit chagrined at such a blatant show of emotion in front of another man, Ethan swiped the back of his hand across each cheek. "Just your blessing would be nice, sir."

"You've got that." Marcus extended his right hand. Ethan

grasped the older man's forearm below the elbow. At the instant of contact, Marcus pulled Ethan into his arms. Warmth flooded Ethan's soul, and the door to his heart swung open, allowing his father to slip inside.

As the two men parted, they gave each other a hearty slap on the back. "We've got a lot of catching up to do," Marcus said.

"Yes, sir. . .Father, we do. But if you don't mind, right now, I'd like to kiss my wife."

Before Ethan could turn to Lillian, she was in his arms, smothering him with a kiss that left his knees weak and his insides jerking. Feeling like a man who'd just been raised from the dead, Ethan wrapped his arms around his wife and drank his fill of her sweet, teary lips.

"Oh, well," he heard Marcus say. "I, uh, guess I'll go back to the camp. I understand I've got another daughter and a couple of grandkids to meet."

He also had a third grandchild on the way, but Ethan figured that introduction could wait a little bit longer.

When they finally ended the kiss, Ethan picked up his wife and spun her around. The sounds of their laughter rose and danced on the wind, spreading renewed joy throughout The Blue Haven.

&

The following morning, Ethan, Lillian, and the rest of the Walker family accompanied Marcus and Frederick to their mounts.

"Do you have to leave so soon, Papa?" Lillian asked, stepping forward to grasp Marcus's hands.

"I'm afraid I do, Princess. I have to get back to my duties."

Disappointment cast a shadow over Lillian's face. "Then you're going to assist in the removal?"

"Yes, but only because I want to do everything within my power to make the remainder of the roundup and the transportation west as easy as possible for the Cherokee." He slid his gaze to Ethan. "I hope that doesn't offend you."

"I appreciate anything you can do for my people," Ethan said, extending his right arm. Marcus grasped it below the elbow.

Marcus moved on to Snowbird, and Ethan once again noticed a deep look of longing settle in his father's eyes—an expression that was mirrored in his mother's. What did the future hold for them? Would Marcus and Snowbird have a chance to recapture the happiness they'd been deprived of twenty-seven years ago? Or was it too late? Ethan released a long sigh of resignation. Only God and Time had the answers to those questions.

Ethan slipped his arm around his wife, thanking God for the precious gift of her love, and silently asking God to some-day give his mother and father an opportunity to experience what he and Lillian now shared, whether it be with each other, or someone else.

Once everyone had said their good-byes, The Pathfinder stepped forward. In one hand, he held an eagle feather wand, a fan of eagle tail feathers attached to a long, thin stick. "I pray that someday our people will be able to live together in harmony," he said in his native tongue.

"And I pray for the same," Marcus returned in Cherokee.

Ethan couldn't help smiling when Lillian's mouth dropped open in surprise.

The Pathfinder brushed Marcus's body with the feather wand, indicating he accepted Marcus as a friend and family. Marcus, in turn, accepted the wand from the aged chief and returned the gesture.

As Marcus and Frederick rode away, a shadow passed over Ethan. He looked up to find a majestic eagle soaring high above the trees, free and unfettered. Once his people had just as freely roamed their native realm. But, over the years, the cruel hands of greed and prejudice had robbed them of their land and almost crushed their humble spirit. Almost.

"But they that wait upon the Lord shall renew their

strength; they shall mount up with wings as eagles; they shall run, and not be weary; and they shall walk, and not faint."

The verse Ethan had recently memorized drifted into his mind, and like a downpour after a long summer drought, peace beyond understanding flooded his soul.

That's exactly what God had done for him; renewed his spirit, given him the strength to go on, and given him the desire to fight to make the world a better place for his wife, his children, and his people.

Thank You, God, for all You've done for me. For replacing my heart of stone with one of flesh, for my precious wife and our unborn child, for my father. . .

As blessing after blessing rolled through Ethan's mind, laughter bubbled up from his chest and escaped his throat. He may have lost a lot, but in return, he'd been given so much.

When his mirth began to ebb, he looked down to find his wife staring at him like he'd lost his mind.

"What was that all about?" she asked.

"Peace," he said, then banished her confused expression with a long, lingering kiss.

authors note

THE END. . . ?
Not yet.

What does the future hold for Ethan's twin sister, Emily? Find out in *Tears in a Bottle* coming from **Heartsong Presents** in Spring of 2001.

A Letter To Our Readers

Dear Reader:

In order that we might better contribute to your reading enjoyment, we would appreciate your taking a few minutes to respond to the following questions. We welcome your comments and read each form and letter we receive. When completed, please return to the following:

Rebecca Germany, Fiction Editor
Heartsong Presents
PO Box 719
Uhrichsville, Ohio 44683

1. Did you enjoy reading *Spirit of the Eagle?*
   ☐ Very much. I would like to see more books
     by this author!
   ☐ Moderately
     I would have enjoyed it more if _____
     _____
     _____

2. Are you a member of **Heartsong Presents**? Yes ☐ No ☐
   If no, where did you purchase this book?_____
   _____

3. How would you rate, on a scale from 1 (poor) to 5 (superior), the cover design?_____

4. On a scale from 1 (poor) to 10 (superior), please rate the following elements.

   _____ Heroine   _____ Plot

   _____ Hero   _____ Inspirational theme

   _____ Setting   _____ Secondary characters

5. These characters were special because_____

_____

_____

6. How has this book inspired your life?_____

_____

_____

7. What settings would you like to see covered in future **Heartsong Presents** books?_____

_____

_____

8. What are some inspirational themes you would like to see treated in future books?_____

_____

_____

9. Would you be interested in reading other **Heartsong Presents** titles?   Yes ❏   No ❏

10. Please check your age range:
    ❏ Under 18   ❏ 18-24   ❏ 25-34
    ❏ 35-45   ❏ 46-55   ❏ Over 55

11. How many hours per week do you read?_____

Name _____

Occupation _____

Address _____

City _____ State _____ Zip _____

·········Presents·········

Great Inspirational Romance at a Great Price!

Heartsong Presents books are inspirational romances in contemporary and historical settings, designed to give you an enjoyable, spirit-lifting reading experience. You can choose wonderfully written titles from some of today's best authors like Peggy Darty, Sally Laity, Tracie Peterson, Colleen L. Reece, Lauraine Snelling, and many others.

When ordering quantities less than twelve, above titles are $2.95 each.
Not all titles may be available at time of order.

Heart♥ng Presents
Love Stories Are Rated G!

That's for godly, gratifying, and of course, great! If you love a thrilling love story, but don't appreciate the sordidness of some popular paperback romances, **Heartsong Presents** is for you. In fact, **Heartsong Presents** is the *only inspirational romance book club* featuring love stories where Christian faith is the primary ingredient in a marriage relationship.

Sign up today to receive your first set of four, never before published Christian romances. Send no money now; you will receive a bill with the first shipment. You may cancel at any time without obligation, and if you aren't completely satisfied with any selection, you may return the books for an immediate refund.

Imagine. . .four new romances every four weeks—two historical, two contemporary—with men and women like you who long to meet the one God has chosen as the love of their lives. . . all for the low price of $9.97 postpaid.

To join, simply complete the coupon below and mail to the address provided. **Heartsong Presents** romances are rated G for another reason: They'll arrive *Godspeed!*
